Past Crimes

Past Crimes

Carol Matas

KEY PORTER BOOKS

Library and Archives Canada Cataloguing in Publication

Matas, Carol, 1949-
    Past crimes / Carol Matas.

ISBN 1-55263-841-3

    I. Title.

PS8576.A7994P37 2006   jC813'.54   C2006-903137-1

The Canada Council | Le Conseil des Arts
  for the arts | du Canada
  since 1957 | depuis 1957

ONTARIO ARTS COUNCIL
CONSEIL DES ARTS DE L'ONTARIO

The publisher gratefully acknowledges the support of the Canada Council for the Arts and
the Ontario Arts Council for its publishing program. We acknowledge the support of the
Government of Ontario through the Ontario Media Development Corporation's Ontario
Book Initiative.

We acknowledge the financial support of the Government of Canada through the Book
Publishing Industry Development Program (BPIDP) for our publishing activities.

This book is printed on acid-free paper that is Ancient Forest Friendly (100% post-consumer
recycled paper).

Key Porter Books Limited
Six Adelaide Street East, Tenth Floor
Toronto, Ontario
Canada M5C 1H6

www.keyporter.com

Text design and formatting: Marijke Friesen

Printed and bound in Canada

06 07 08 09 10 5 4 3 2 1

To my Kobrinsky godchildren:
Isaac, Sarah, Leah, Aryeh, Yehudah, and Zach

and to
Cassandre and Clotilde Aras

Love you all!

Acknowledgements

Special thanks to Peter Atwood for all his help on this book, and to Perry Nodelman and my husband, Per Brask, for their insights. Linda Pruessen, my editor, has been a pleasure to work with and made the revisions almost seem easy—quite a feat! And thanks to David Bennett, my agent, for everything he does. The poems are written by Per Brask.

1.

Screams.

The sounds are like women's voices, but at this level of fear, that high-pitched screech, like an animal caught in a trap, could be male or female. Where am I? I don't even know if I am inside or outside. I look up. No roof. Stars overhead. I look down. I am standing on a small wood platform. Smoke is snaking up through the slats. Soon it will be in full blaze. I am wearing a thick long skirt. Flames begin to lick the bottom of it. I need to run, but I cannot. Something is holding me. My hands are tied. . . . A scream escapes my throat, adding my voice to the others.

⁓

"Mrs. Green. Mrs. Green."

My eyes flew open.

A woman so tiny I could almost see through her was standing over me. She looked like a ten-year-old who had dressed up in a nurse's uniform for Halloween. Her black hair was pulled into a ponytail and her hand was cold on my wrist. She spoke slowly and clearly as if to a child. "Mrs. Green. Mrs. Green. You are in the hospital. You have been shot."

Shot?

Okay. I understood what the word meant, but not how it related to *me*. This made no sense. I stared at her, as if I could get the gist of what she was saying if I simply stared hard enough. My head was spinning and I felt like I was about to throw up, but I didn't have time for that. I tried to focus.

"You were lucky, though." The nurse was still talking. "The bullet hit the muscle in your left arm. The surgeons have repaired it and they think you should regain full function. You'll be fine in no time." She paused. "Another bullet grazed your head, probably knocked you out, but there's no serious damage. A few stitches, that's all."

"Most likely what saved your life." I'd been so busy trying to concentrate on the nurse that I hadn't noticed anyone else in the room. The voice was deep and rich. I followed the sound, turned my head—which produced a searing, shooting pain right through my skull—and found myself looking over at a tall, lean man with chiseled features and a shock of black hair. His eyes were a bright blue and softened his face a little. He had a notepad in his hand.

"Nate." My voice was so hoarse it came out as a whisper. I was finally starting to come around and of course it was Nate I thought about first.

"Your friend, Beth, has your baby with her," the nurse answered. "Don't worry. She found you and called the ambulance. She told me to tell you he's already sound asleep."

"Rosaline Green?" the man said.

"Ros," I corrected him automatically.

"Detective Pauls, Mrs. Green," he said. "I need to interview you while things are still fresh in your mind."

The nurse took my pulse and blood pressure while he stood there waiting for me to speak. Fresh in my mind? My mind was a mess. I felt awful. My head was swimming and everything they'd just told me sounded ridiculous, and made me think I was still dreaming.

And then, suddenly, the whole thing came back to me.

∽

I stepped out of the shower and toweled off, trying not to look in the mirror. *It's not a date or anything,* I scolded myself. *He's not going to see you naked. Stop it!*

But the more I tried to quiet that incessant voice, the more impossible it became. I gave up, dropped the towel and stared: a mane of curly red hair flowing over my shoulders, green eyes, freckles everywhere—and I mean everywhere—long legs, ribs sticking out . . . that's what I saw. I sighed, trying not to remember Saul's reaction whenever he saw me naked.

Anyway, I was going out with a friend from university, Jordan, and his dad, for heaven's sake—not even close to a date! So why the panic? Of course, when I took Nate next door to Beth's she teased me mercilessly. "All ready for your date?"

"It's not a date!" I insisted.

"It's a disguised date," she smiled. She hugged Nate before letting him run into the playroom off the living room, shrieking with delight when he saw Lisa. He barely gave me a backward glance. "Jordan would have asked you out already if he'd thought there was a chance you'd say yes. The family thing is just a way to get things rolling."

"You're trying to freak me out, aren't you?" I said.

"I think it's time you got out there," she said, her tone more serious. "What's so terrible about a date?"

I didn't answer. How soon after you lose the love of your life is too soon?

She shook her head when she saw the look on my face and gave me a little shove. "Oh, go get ready," she said.

Jordan was at the house just after seven—well, Jordan, his dad and his two brothers. Jordan's dad is great. He's an obstetrician and he also volunteers at the family planning clinic, as do I. I met so many young kids when I was pregnant, and some of them weren't coping at all. A few were even drinking and doing drugs, heavy-duty drugs, and I wished someone would have counselled them about their options. When I moved here I decided to volunteer a bit of my time to do just that. Advice comes easier from someone close to your own age.

Anyway, Jordan's dad always has a joke—and funny ones, no less. Not like my dad. He always has jokes, too—lame ones. Jordan is painfully shy in comparison. He's in my Jewish history class, and he was so shy about talking in class, which we get marked on, that I took pity on him and asked him out for coffee one day to give him some tips on participating. I told him that, if he wanted to, he could just pretend he was talking to me. It seemed to help, although maybe it was just knowing that everyone wasn't ready to make fun of him. Turns out he wants to study biblical literacy and is taking Hebrew, Aramaic and Greek so he can read the bible in its original languages. Okay, he's a bit geeky, but in a nice way. I like him.

It was his dad, though, that asked me to come along to Jordan's birthday dinner. He said that if I didn't there would be four boys and they needed a female. I'm not sure what the story is with Jordan's mom, except that she and his dad are divorced and I gather there's a bit of a freeze between them. Maybe he was just taking pity on me since my parents are gone—my dad's the guest scholar at a university in Sydney, Australia, the trip of a lifetime—and I've been feeling pretty lonely. Or maybe he was trying to set me and Jordan up. Who knows?

We went to Santa Lucia. It's one of my favourite restaurants, but one I couldn't afford on my own. Even my parents can't afford it lately, what with taking me and Nate in and sending me to university. The price of diapers alone for a one-year-old amounts to a dinner out. My poor parents. They might have thought that, at nineteen, I'd still be living at home, but I doubt they'd ever have imagined that I'd have a baby as well.

I stuffed myself with cannelloni, salad and manicotti, all of it perfectly delicious. Dr. Graham had more silly jokes than usual, and the boys chatted away about the coming baseball season. Between us there were Angels fans, Dodger fans and one, Jordan, who couldn't care less.

On the way home Dr. Graham opened the sunroof. It was the middle of March and the weather was mild, we still hadn't had a really severe hot spell. I tilted my head back as we drove and looked at the stars. It was a beautiful night. The air was warm, and smelled of roses and lemon blossoms. Jordan was sitting beside me. We made small talk about the classes we'd both be taking in the summer session, how our studying was going for our finals and what essays we still had to do. We drove down Highway 111, the main artery that connects the desert cities: Palm Springs, Cathedral City, Rancho Mirage, Palm Desert, La Quinta, and Indio.

My house is in a quiet residential community in Palm Springs, on one of five streets sandwiched between a country club and an old folks' home. I grew up here and the neighbourhood always makes me feel safe and happy. It was around ten when Dr. Graham turned into my driveway. The light by the driveway was out for some reason, and the porch light wasn't on either, although I distinctly remembered turning it on before I left the house. "That's annoying," I said. "I just put a new bulb in over the porch yesterday."

"I'll come over tomorrow and fix it if you want," Jordan said quickly.

I didn't answer. Maybe Beth was right; maybe Jordan did like me. I didn't know what to say, and the last thing I wanted was to hurt his feelings. I really was *not* ready to date yet.

Jordan's father jumped into the awkward pause. "Let's have a look at it right now," he said, opening the car door and getting out. I followed, leaving Jordan and two his brothers in the car.

And then I heard this incredible noise, so loud, like a car backfiring. Dr. Graham's eyes opened wide then and he screamed—a horrible sound of pure agony. He slumped forward onto the hood of the car. And then my arm felt like someone had just burned it and something hit my head and everything went black.

〜

I looked at the nurse. "Dr. Graham? Jordan?" I asked.

"Dr. Graham took a more serious hit than you. He's still in surgery."

"You were lucky," the detective added. "The bullet that grazed you appeared to have hit you square in the head. The shooter must've figured you for dead. The boys weren't hurt."

Perhaps I was still dreaming. But that had been different—smoke, fire? Pain suddenly ripped through my arm. I looked down to see it swathed in bandages. I was hooked up to tons of machines and had too many tubes coming out of me to count.

"We'll be moving you into a room on the surgical ward in a bit," the nurse said. "You're in recovery now. Most of those tubes will come out then."

"I can only stay a minute more," Detective Pauls said. "I just needed to find out if you saw anyone, if you know the shooter. Then we can get after him or her before it's too late."

I shook my head. Big mistake. I gasped in pain.

"You didn't see *anyone?*" he asked again.

"No one," I managed to answer.

"I'll drop by tomorrow," he said. When he left, I closed my eyes. I needed to make sense of this. I needed to think.

∽

I am on a street flooded with sunlight. Flowers spill from the sidewalk planters onto the pavement: reds and pinks and yellows and oranges; bougainvillea, snapdragons and California poppies. I am running as fast as I can. I have to find Saul. I have to find him before it's too late. I need to warn him. I need to stop it from happening. And there he is, standing under a Washington palm. His arms are open. I fly into them and he strokes my hair. I feel the warmth of his body, smell his scent, breath it in as I clasp him to me.

"It's too late for me," he whispers into my thick hair, holding me tight. "But not for him."

"Him?"

"Nate."

My heart freezes with fear.

2.

That feeling of dread from the dream was still with me when I woke. The nurse was gone now. The machines made little beeping noises and I could hear voices out in the hallway, muted. But I was alone. Too alone. I wished the nurse would come back. Even that detective. I wished my parents were here. Most of all, I wished Saul was here.

And then, I suppose because of the dream, I suddenly remembered a day on the beach. A beautiful day when Saul was still alive and the world made sense. Or I thought it did.

It was summer. We were walking on the boardwalk in San Diego, where we'd gone to celebrate shortly after we'd found out we were pregnant. A small cloud covered the sun.

"Look," said Saul.

He took his sunglasses off, then put them back on, then took them off again, all the time looking at the sun-covered cloud. Then he passed them to me and told me to try.

Without glasses the cloud looked white. With them, a vivid rainbow appeared all around the cloud's edges.

"There's so much that we don't see, isn't there?" he said softly.

"What do you mean?" I asked.

"I don't know," he said. "Maybe it's the fact that we'll soon be parents. It's such a miracle—to create a life. It's so amazing. I'm thinking the world might be more spectacular than I ever imagined."

I threw myself into his arms and we kissed, the wind gentle around us, the sun warm on our skin, and the baby just starting to make itself known to me.

But as it so often did, this happy memory immediately brought with it the other memory, the one I was never far away from: the moment the police came to the door to tell me about Saul. It was his partner, a fellow I didn't know too well yet since they'd only been on the force a few months. His name, Bert. I always wondered if he'd been named after the *Sesame Street* Bert because he looked exactly like him. Just seeing him made me giggle. Not this time, though. Nate had just gone down for his nap, and so had I, and I was mad when I got to the door, disoriented and angry about being woken up. I hadn't believed Bert at first. I'd thought it was some elaborate sick joke. Saul was famous for his practical jokes. I realized later that Saul never would have done anything so cruel—he didn't have a mean bone in his body—but at the time it seemed more believable than his being shot. Than his being *dead*.

Not counting a short breakup in my final year of high school, Saul and I had been together from the spring of tenth grade. I was fifteen years old then, and my parents were a little uncomfortable with me seeing someone two and a half years older. On the other hand, it was Saul—my brother's best friend, and almost one of the family. Since I'd accelerated, we were only a year apart at school. My friends, like Susana, got it right away. I mean, they just had to hang out with us and they'd get all jealous and wonder why couldn't they find someone like Saul, someone who wasn't an immature jerk and wasn't always on the make, who wasn't either a jock or a geek, someone who was just *himself*. Of course, the other great catch was my brother—Saul's best friend—but he was a bit flighty back then and went through girls like a major leaguer goes through bats.

When Saul died his parents made all the funeral arrangements; I was basically a basket case. After I'd returned to Palm Springs for the funeral it occurred to me that I should just stay. My parents were still here, so were his (although they've since moved to be near their daughter and three other grandchildren), and I hoped that if we returned we'd be safe. After all, I knew the town. It was small and manageable, and I would always have a handle on what was happening. There was something else as well. The hot sun, the wide expanses of white sand, the mountains all around seemed suddenly precious—part of me and Saul when we were happy and carefree. And in a way I wanted to be the child, to live at home again, to be taken care of, to feel that safety I used to feel.

That was just over a year ago. Nate was two months old. Two months. Saul had changed his diapers, had gotten up at night with him, had loved him to pieces. . . .

The police still haven't caught Saul's killer, though they say they're still looking. He was one of them, after all, a policeman shot in an alley—maybe by an informer he used? He'd only graduated from police training months earlier, after taking a two-year university course in Los Angeles. I'd taken a job at Starbucks to help support him and had managed to work almost right up to Nate's birth. I was going to go back to school eventually, but we figured we'd have babies first, while we were young. Once they were in school I'd go back. We had all these plans. Then someone snatched them away from us. Someone.

And now what was happening?

I must have slept again, not waking until the staff came to move me out of ICU.

"How do you feel?" the nurse asked.

"Not too bad," I replied, although I actually felt like I'd been run over by a truck. Everything hurt. "What hospital am I in?"

"White Sands. Doctors are due for rounds in about half an hour."

They moved me to a semi-private room, settling me in just in time for rounds. I gathered that White Sands is a teaching hospital when the surgeon—Dr. Strong—came in with a string of students trailing after him. He was an older man; round, with a ring of white hair circling a bald head, a round face, a round stomach, even rounded hands. His appearance reminded me of a cheerful gnome, but his expression said the opposite. He looked at my chart, explained the surgery to the students, and asked quick questions about my pain.

"Will my arm be normal again?" I asked him.

"No doubt it will, Mrs. Green," he said as he turned back to his students and made his way out of the room. "More than she deserves," he said under his breath.

Had I heard that right? I watched as he and his students moved off. I must have misunderstood. . . .

꩜

Detective Pauls came in a little after 8 a.m. "You look much better," he said. I knew right then he was nice. I must've looked like hell. The woman in the bed next to me had had a bad night, moaning and groaning. I wasn't sure why she was there, but I could see she was very old. Maybe ninety—like really old. She couldn't hear properly and the nurses had to almost scream when they talked to her. I don't think I slept at all.

"Remember anything else?" he asked.

"Nothing."

"We're checking every angle," he assured me. "So far, no leads, but it's early days." I was struck again by the sheer force of his presence, his deep voice and those piercing eyes. I was glad he was on my side. "We're still working the crime scene," he added.

24

The front of my house. The place I thought was safe. What if I had been killed? Nate would have been left an orphan. Suddenly I burst out crying, terrible, deep wrenching sobs. I felt Detective Pauls put a hand on my shoulder. A few moments later a nurse was there, trying to calm me down. But nothing was working. The sobs turned to hiccups and I couldn't stop. Somehow I'd grabbed the detective's hand and now I couldn't let go. The tears felt hot on my cheeks and his hand felt hot on my shoulder. I gasped for breath. I heard Dr. Strong's voice in the background, and saw the nurse approach me with a needle. I felt her give it to me, knowing it was a sedative, and knowing I needed it.

Late that afternoon, I woke to a call from my brother, Jon. Beth had contacted him, he said. He offered to fly out, but I said no. He had a new baby at home and I knew Marsha needed him. I begged him not to call Mom and Dad, either. They'd looked forward to this trip for so long and I didn't want to ruin it. I told him I'd call them myself in the next day or so if I needed them to come home. He hung up then, promising to call me that night to check in.

I put the receiver back in its cradle, fighting the urge to cry. I felt worse than ever, and very sorry for myself. Why had I not accepted Jon's offer? I needed my family. But Mom and Dad were so far away that even if I did call them by the time they got home I'd be practically better, so what was the point? Maybe I *would* ask Jon to come for a day or two. I decided to wait a bit and see how I felt. I picked at my hospital food as I called Beth. Nate was fine, she said, urging me to rest. I hung up and closed my eyes.

The poor woman next to me was gone when I woke around ten. I feared the worst but didn't ask. I had the room to myself and slept almost through the night, except when the nurses came in to poke and prod.

The next morning Dr. Strong checked my dressing, then told the nurse I could be discharged.

Soon after, I found myself in a taxi on my way home. The only thing I was sure about was how desperate I was to see Nate. Everything else seemed lost in a horrible dark fog.

3.

All I could think about on the way home was picking Nate up and holding him tight and never letting go. But when I got there and found him playing on the floor with Beth and Lisa, I couldn't because my arm was too sore. Instead, I gave him lots of hugs and got lots of hugs and kisses back. That almost made me cry again, but I wouldn't let myself fall apart in front of him.

Beth got me settled on the couch and made sure the children were organized in the playpen with their favourite toys. I sighed, grateful for her presence and her friendship. Just after I moved back Beth had arrived in the desert from L.A. with her husband, Chris. He'd accepted a job as an oncologist at Roosevelt

Hospital. She's a doctor, too—a pediatrician—but with a new baby at home she decided to take a few years off. They'd moved into the house next door and we'd immediately liked each other. She started dropping over after dinner, when her husband was called to the hospital and she'd be left with a colicky baby. "Even working thirty-six hours straight as a resident," she'd said, "can't compare with a baby with a tummy ache."

Beth is older than me, twenty-seven, but that has never really mattered. I guess it's like having an older sister. We're pretty different in many ways. Beth believes devoutly in a higher power and in all things strange and wonderful. She loved *The X Files*, for instance. I tease her about this—about a scientist behaving so unscientifically. She's a lapsed Roman Catholic, and is quick to explain that she was raised with a belief in evil spirits, possessions, and miracles. She believes in dreams, in psychic abilities, in, well, in everything. Her favourite quote is from Hamlet: "There are more things in heaven and earth, Horatio, Than are dreamt of in your philosophy."

I don't really have a set of "beliefs." My parents are Reform Jews and have always worried more about the here and now than the there and whatever. I did go to Hebrew school, and I had a bat mitzvah, but I've never worried too much about God or why things happen.

At least not until Saul was killed. And then, when I did think about God, it wasn't in any kind of friendly way. I had trouble at Saul's funeral service, for instance. In a Jewish funeral, the mourners praise God. But I didn't think God *should* be praised. I let others say those prayers. If I had done anything that day, it would have been to curse, not praise. But I prefer to think that there is no "One" in charge. Then I don't have to be mad at any One. Beth likes to talk about these "spiritual" things, but I try to avoid the topic as much as possible.

Anyway, my real bond with Beth is the kids. Lisa is just two months older than Nate, who's fourteen months now. As soon as they were old enough to play together they were inseparable. Lisa started walking and talking while Nate was still babbling and trying to walk. Lisa cries easily, while Nate has to do far more than bonk his head on a hard object before he cries. Lisa is an average height and Nate is tall. But they're both very sociable and very sweet, and they get along famously. And how great is it that whenever Nate gets sick Beth tells me what's wrong without a long wait in a doctor's office—especially since they almost always get sick together.

When Beth came back to the living room with a cup of tea in hand, she seemed concerned. She had her blonde hair tied back off her face and looked more like eighteen than twenty-seven, her skin shining with a natural pink glow. When we were out together people assumed we were friends of the same age.

"I've noticed a police car drive past twice now," she said. "I'd sort of assumed the target was Dr. Graham, but maybe the police are worried you're still in danger."

As if on cue the doorbell rang and soon Beth was showing Detective Pauls in.

"You seem much improved, Mrs. Green," he said. He had an unsettling way of looking right at you with those intense blue eyes. I let my own gaze wander toward the window.

"I feel better now that I'm home," I answered. "Beth thinks your men are watching the house. Are they?" I looked back at him.

"Well, we don't know yet if you're still in danger. A patrol car is just driving by every once in a while. Better safe than sorry."

"Thank you," I said, although knowing that a maniac could still be out there gunning for me made me feel queasy. Was I putting Nate at risk just having him with me? Again, I got a sense that I was in some kind of bizarre dream and I only needed to wake up. None of this made any sense. I'd have screamed in frustration if I'd had the energy.

"I need you to think, Mrs. Green," he said, "about who might have done this. Have you had any serious fights with anyone?"

I though about it for a minute but couldn't come up with anything. I looked at Beth.

"Oh, I'm sorry, Detective. This is my friend Beth Lawrence. Beth, can you think of anything?"

She shook her head.

"I'm sorry to have to tell you this," he said after a long and awkward pause, "but Dr. Graham didn't pull through. He died an hour ago."

I stared at him for a moment, unable to take it in.

Oddly, the first thought I had was for Saul. And it was more a feeling than a thought. I was angry. *How could you have left me alone like this? How can I keep Nate safe when I can't even protect myself?* I felt a tear trickle down my cheek. I had used up all my strength trying to survive Saul's death. I had none left for this.

And poor Dr. Graham. He had been so nice. What about Jordan and his brothers, left alone, like Nate, with no dad? Beth sat beside me on the couch and held my hand.

"We're not sure if you were the target or if he was," he continued. "The only thing that ties you together is the family clinic. He did abortions there, I understand, and you do counselling?"

I nodded. "Are you telling me it was one of those fanatics? Someone from a right-to-life group?"

"I'm not saying that, no. We have no theories yet. Dr. Graham's son, Jordan, also ties you together," he said. "I'll let you know if we come up with something. But I need you to think hard—about anyone who might hold a grudge." He paused for a moment and looked around the living room.

"Are you and your son living here on your own?"

"It's my parents' house," I answered. "But they're away in Australia."

He nodded and put a card on the side table. "Call if anything unusual strikes you, anything at all," he said as he turned to leave. For some odd reason, I noticed that he was wearing cowboy boots.

✑

A woman is crying. But it isn't a normal kind of crying, it is a desperate wail. She stands in the centre of a circle of black-coated men. They are speaking to her in low voices, almost like a chant, but I can't hear what they are saying. The woman pleads with them. She is wearing a long skirt and a thick top with long sleeves. Her face is round and ruddy: a good, honest peasant face. The men's faces are thin and white, their hands gesturing with long white fingers that look like tentacles.

༄

I woke up with a gasp.

Beth, who was sitting in a chair beside the couch reading one of my mysteries, put down the book and raised her eyebrows.

"Dreaming?" she said. "Tell me."

I sighed. Beth felt sure that every dream was a message from our higher selves—but some were from *the* higher source itself.

"Both babies are sound asleep," she added, before I even had a chance to ask.

I shook my head, too tired to indulge her. Ever since we became friends Beth's been pulling my dreams out of me. I usually tell her it's just a bunch of neurons firing or too much ice cream before bed. She insists there's a hidden universe just waiting to be tapped, and worse, if we don't pay attention to it we'll be sorry. According to Beth, my dreams are quite amazing and hold all kinds of clues about my life. I tell her I'm not interested in deities that deal in clues, if they're so all powerful, they can send me an email. And they can make it a clear one, too!

In any case, I didn't want to think about it now. I closed my eyes and dropped back into an uneasy sleep.

4.

Dr. Graham's funeral was Wednesday. Only five days had passed since the shooting, but in some ways it felt like forever. Although I was still weak and my arm still bandaged, I was determined to go. Beth offered to look after Nate, so I called Susana and she agreed to drive me. Susana is one of the few high school friends that I stayed in touch with when Saul and I moved to L.A. We don't have a lot in common these days, what with our different lifestyles, but we've managed to remain friends. Susana's a real adventurer. She took over the Palm Springs branch of her mom's clothing store right out of high school and flies all over the world on buying trips. She has no time for a significant other, never mind babies. I'm in first year university and still have no idea what I want to do with my life. Susana's all set.

She arrived in her hybrid Lexus suv, dressed elegantly in a grey designer suit, her long, glossy black hair swinging easily from a perfect cut, her dark eyes full of worry for me. Every time I saw her I was amazed at what a beauty she was, and yet she seemed to have no idea of her effect on others, especially guys.

The funeral was being held at St. Anthony's Church in Palm Desert—a magnificent two-storey whitewashed structure with a bell tower, surrounded by palm trees. We sat down near the back, but even so I noticed heads craning and a small buzz of conversation that started up when we came in. After all, I'd been with him when it happened. Were these people thinking that it was lucky I was alive to attend his funeral? I thought the same. I wondered if I should go to the front, where Jordan must be sitting with his mom and brothers. But after hearing that buzz I didn't want to draw any more attention to myself.

The service started. Dr. Graham's sister gave a moving speech about him, as did a colleague from the hospital. Then Jordan's younger brother, Ken, spoke. He's tall, with short brown hair parted down the middle and a noticeable case of acne. He'll probably be good looking, once he's finished with the awkwardness of being a teen.

"I don't understand," he began, "how a person who believes in life can take a life. I don't understand." The crowd shifted uncomfortably. I was pretty surprised that Ken was being so brutally frank and honest. But I remember thinking when we were out for dinner that he was way more outspoken than Jordan. But I was also surprised that he assumed it was an anti-abortion nut. Did they know something I didn't? "My dad loved his work," he continued. "Sometimes so much he didn't have time for us. But if a baby needed to be delivered it didn't matter that one of us had a ball game. It didn't matter if it was in the middle of a birthday party."

The crowd murmured.

"It didn't matter because the baby couldn't wait, could it? He—-we—gave up a lot. He didn't deserve to be killed. No one was more dedicated to babies, or to their moms.

"I just want the murderer to know," he continued, "that he's taken a life—a life that's probably done more good than that creep could ever hope to do. He's the evil one, not my dad. Evil."

Ken stopped abruptly and sat down.

Next, Jordan's older brother, Stephen, came to the microphone. He was clear skinned and his face was rounder. He too, was tall and athletic looking. He stood for a moment, as if uncertain what to say.

"My dad used to say that everything comes from God," he said quietly. "That must mean even the killer does."

He sat down. I think what he said stunned everyone even more than what his brother had said. It certainly stunned me. How could he be so forgiving? It made me feel even worse. Some maniac had taken these great kids—had taken their lives—and wrecked them without a thought. I knew one thing for sure: the only person the killer cared about was himself. Or herself.

I found I was trembling from head to foot. We sang some hymns and finally the service was over.

"Should we go?" asked Susana.

"I have to put in an appearance at the reception," I answered. It was being held in the church basement. Susana took my arm and because we were at the back we were among the first into the hall.

I went straight to Jordan and took his hand with my good one and told him how sorry I was. He looked done in—his face pale, his longish hair tangled, his eyes red from crying. He asked if I was all right. I shrugged, not really knowing how to answer. People were starting to crowd around us so I spoke to his brothers, and then I introduced myself to Jordan's mom.

She was a tall woman in her early forties with short brown hair, brown eyes, high cheekbones, and an olive complexion. She wore square, large glasses and was dressed in a smart black suit.

"Ros Green," she said, her eyes cold and hard. "A pity my husband was with you when it happened."

I stared at her, confused.

"Think about it," she continued, "it didn't happen at home, did it? Or at the clinic. Or at the hospital. I think the bullets were meant for you and my husband got in the way."

I was speechless. Thankfully, Susana was not.

"Mrs. Graham, I am terribly sorry for your loss," she said. "My name is Susana Izquierdo, and I'm an old friend of Ros's. The only thing that connects your husband and Ros is their work at the abortion clinic. I don't think it matters where it happened, does it? They were probably followed from the clinic."

If that were true, I suddenly thought, why was the light out at my house? Why was the murderer waiting for us? I stared open-mouthed at Dr. Graham's wife. Were the police not telling me something? Was there more to this than was evident? And why did she obviously hate me? I could see it in her eyes.

Maybe *she* did it, I thought to myself, stifling a mental giggle. The strain of the day was obviously beginning to tell. I almost laughed aloud right there and then. I turned and left, hanging on to Susana for dear life, all the time gritting my teeth to stop a burst of hysterical laughter.

We were about to go out the door when we nearly bumped into a small, unnaturally thin woman who shrieked with delight when she saw me. She had a long face, a sharp nose, and light brown hair cut in a bob and streaked with blond. She wore way too much makeup—bright green eyeshadow and a ton of mascara—which made her look older than she actually probably was. The look was completed with a bright pink suit, hardly befitting the occasion. She looked vaguely familiar but I couldn't place her at first, although she obviously knew me.

"Ros! Oh my God! Thank heavens you are all right! And after what happened to Saul!"

I wracked my brain, trying to think. Who was this? I hated this feeling. Since I'd returned to the desert, I often bumped into old school chums who seemed to have perfect memories—they all knew and remembered me, along with every other person they'd gone to school with. I, on the other hand, remembered only the ones who had really been friends. I could tell that she was realizing I had no clue who she was.

"Maureen, it's been a while since Ros has seen you," Susana chided. "You could at least remind a person...."

Susana always felt that going on the offensive was a much better tack than going in the defensive.

"Of course, you're right," Maureen said, hitting her forehead in a mock display of stupidity. "But I just assumed Ros would remember *me*...." For a moment, I thought I saw a strange glint in her eye, but it was gone so quickly I wondered whether I'd imagined it.

Maureen. Well, now I did remember. In grade twelve, when Saul and I broke up, he'd briefly gone out with Maureen. She'd been crazy about him. In fact, she'd stopped me in the hall one day at school and asked me if we were really through. I was so mad at him at the time that I'd said we were—for sure. She'd confided that she'd had a crush on Saul for as long as she could remember. Even though he'd graduated a year earlier, she said that she'd never forgotten him. If it was okay with me, she was going to ask him out. I said that it was, although the sinking feeling that hit my stomach when the words crossed my lips told me that I was still nuts about him.

A slight blush came to my cheeks as I remembered what happened next. Not my proudest moment. Or Saul's. I'd gone to the graduation dance with my friend, Phil. Saul had said yes when Maureen asked him out, and he showed up at the dance with her. We met at the drinks counter. He took my hand.

"One dance," he'd said, his voice quiet but so convincing. I looked into his eyes and couldn't imagine why we'd ever broken up. (It had been a stupid fight over Phil, actually. Saul had been jealous about our friendship.) I followed him to the dance floor. He took me in his arms. I lay my head on his shoulder. We kissed.

And all our friends started clapping. When Saul looked for Maureen later, she'd gone. I don't think I'd seen her from that day to this.

"Of course," I said. "Maureen Daly."

"I'm so sorry about Saul," she said. "So sad. And now Jordan's dad. Had you known him long?"

"A while," I answered.

"You must promise to let me take you out for lunch one day," she said. "We can catch up on old times."

We were never very good friends so I wasn't sure what old times she meant.

"Ros is still very tired, Maureen," Susana said. "I'm taking her home."

"Of course, of course," Maureen said as she stepped aside. "I'll call you," she added.

As we got outside, Susana grimaced, "She never says she'll call me. I'm insulted, to say the least. And I knew her better than you did."

"What is she up to these days?" I asked.

"She sells real estate."

I had to laugh.

"I hope," Susana sniffed, with mock horror, "that you are not laughing at real estate agents."

"No," I said, "heaven forbid. But she just looks like she sells real estate. It's too perfect."

"You are!" Susana accused me. "You are categorizing all real estate agents. I'm sure some are very nice. Maureen is very good at it, too," Susana added. "She's heading toward being millionaire, I'll bet. And you have something to thank her for already."

"What's that?"

"She made you laugh."

I shook my head. "I feel like I don't deserve to ever laugh again. I feel so guilty. Why did it never occur to me that I could be putting myself in danger by working at the clinic?"

"I could see you feeling that way if you were doing the abortions," Susana said. "Or even if you were a nurse. But volunteering. . . . how would anyone even know you were involved?"

"They must have been watching the clinic," I said.

She nodded. "Anyway, let the police handle it. You just get better."

"It is odd, though, isn't it, that they came to my house," I said, thinking about what Dr. Graham's wife had said.

"With nutcases, nothing is odd," Susana replied. And we drove home.

5.

The smell of burnt flesh is everywhere. Blood curdling screams reach from earth right into the heavens. I am in a cell. I feel I will choke. I am so terrified all I can do is whimper. The cell has a small window high up and a stream of light illuminates the cracked earth of the floor. There is an ant colony working diligently in the centre of the cell and I try to watch it in an attempt to block out the sounds and the smells. It doesn't work.

∽

I woke up gasping for air, dripping in sweat. It was the middle of the night. A cool breeze filled with the scent of lemon blossoms was blowing through the open window, and the drapes ballooned in and out with the gusts. My heart was thudding so hard I had to get out of bed. I shut the window and double-checked the lock. I never should have left it open. I walked up and down the hall, the tiles cold on my bare feet. I checked on Nate who was fast asleep, his arm flung around his favourite stuffed tiger. After a bit, I decided to make myself some hot chocolate. I knew I'd never get back to sleep.

My bedroom and Nate's are on one side of the house, with a bathroom between them. My parents' bedroom and bath are on the other side of the living room, dining room, and kitchen. The house was quiet as I walked. I heard the crickets outside and the wind rustling the palm fronds. Despite the calm around me, my heart wouldn't stop racing. I put my hand on my chest as if that might help. Once in the kitchen I made sure that all the window coverings were closed up tight, and then flipped all the lights on. I tuned the satellite radio to the new music station and made hot chocolate. I sat down at the kitchen table.

I missed my mom and dad. I missed Saul, too, of course, but I was used to that. But right then, I felt like a little kid again, and I wanted Mommy to make my hot chocolate, just as she did that night I woke up to find the big bad wolf standing at the end of my bed.

Whichever way I looked, there he was. I had never been so terrified. I finally made a break for my parents' room—and Mom made me hot chocolate. Apparently I'd had a waking dream.

I thought about the dreams I'd been having lately. They were all about the same thing—some kind of fire and burning—and each one seemed to build on the last. That wasn't normal was it? Telling a story like a movie or a novel in your dreams? It certainly had never happened to me before. Maybe if I had time later I'd do an Internet search on dreams and see what turned up. I smiled as the sound of my dad's voice filled my head. "Go to the library," he would say, "that's what books are for—research, real research." Funny thing, the mind, I thought. Sometimes what you imagine can seem more real than what is actually real. I mean, I still couldn't believe I'd been shot. In a way, the wolf dream seemed more real to me than that.

I realized that it would be daytime in Australia. I stared at the phone. Maybe Mom could come home while Dad stayed and finished his work. I sighed. That would never work. The minute they heard what had happened, they'd both be on the next plane. I'd had to practically force them to go in the first place. I thought of phoning Grandma and Pops in L.A., but what could they do, except worry? There was one thing I could do. First thing in the morning, I'd call a security firm and use the credit card Mom had left for emergencies. If they saw it on their bill and asked me about it, I'd just say I got spooked staying in the house alone.

I turned out the lights and checked in on Nate one last time. Sometime around three or four, I fell asleep. Blissfully, I didn't dream.

I had a class the next morning, and despite the fact that I'd had barely any sleep the night before I wanted to go. Exams were coming up and I had no intention of losing my entire term. I was attending the new university campus in Palm Springs. It had only opened a few years ago. Before that College of the Desert was the highest learning institute here. I enrolled in a general arts program because I really had no idea what I wanted to do. I still don't. I'm good at math and science, but also like English. This term I took English, math, biology, and Jewish studies—the latter because it was the only other class that fit into my schedule. It's ended up being one of the most challenging classes of my year. Our exam was only a few weeks away, and I didn't want to miss the discussion.

I finally felt able to drive, so I took Mom's red Saturn for the trip. First, though, I had to drop Nate off at the synagogue daycare. It's not a perfect arrangement. I'd rather be home with him, but I figure he'd rather have a mom who has a decent job one day than a mom who's on welfare. My mom can't stay with him because she teaches theatre at College of the Desert and Dad drives into Riverside to University of California where he teaches English, especially Shakespeare. They met at Riverside in a drama production of *Much Ado About Nothing*—she played Beatrice and he played Benedick. When he got a job there they decided he'd commute so that their children wouldn't have to grow up in all that smog. That's how we ended up in Palm Springs.

Nate learned to say *Mama* a few months ago, and he said it over and over in the car as I drove down Mesquite— —palm trees swaying in a brisk wind, the sky a fierce blue, and me really wanting to stay glued to him as if that could keep both of us safe. He also tried out his brand new word, *truck*, every time we passed one. *Car*, *tree*, and *flower* were getting plenty of practice as well. Every time he saw something he could name he would shout it with glee, as if it was the first time anyone in the world had ever seen the object. Once at daycare Nate was fine with me leaving. I wish I could say the same.

I slipped into class just as it was starting, hoping to escape notice. As soon as I sat down, however, Barbara—this super-religious evangelical Christian, who often tries to take over—got started before Professor Glass could stop her. "We're all really sorry for what happened, Ros," she said. Barbara was a tall woman with long, dirty blonde hair and pale blue eyes. She is always dressed in long skirts and shapeless tops, giving her the look of either a religious Mormon, a religious Jew, a hippy, or just someone with very bad fashion sense. She was seated beside me. "Don't you think that for something like that to happen, there must be some kind of an entity, you know, *evil*?" She put that question to Professor Glass. Part of our class deals with Jewish philosophy and the Jewish approach to good and evil, so we often discuss these larger themes. Barbara, of course, believes in the devil. As far as I can tell, this isn't exactly a Jewish belief. Well, not in the same sense as Christians, with heaven and hell and fire and brimstone and all that "the devil made me do it" stuff.

"No, Barbara," Professor Glass replied. "I think people make choices. And although we can choose to be selfish and satisfy our needs at the expense of others, we can also choose not to behave that way: 'Love your neighbour as yourself' from Leviticus, 19:18. Both Hillel and Rabbi Akiva—two of the greatest minds in Jewish thought—say *that* is the central theme of Judaism. And," she added, "no one who believes that could be capable of committing this kind of crime. Now if we could return to our topic today—the Inquisition and the persecution of the Jews in Spain and Portugal."

Suddenly from behind me came a familiar voice.

"Can you tell me why people over the ages insist on persecuting other people?"

I turned in my seat to see Jordan standing there clutching his books, face white, eyes red.

"Jordan," said Professor Glass, "We are all so sorry about what happened to your dad." The rest of the class murmured agreement. There was an awkward pause. "You and I can make a special arrangement about the class, and the exam," she said. "Why not come see me after class?"

Jordan stood stubbornly where he was. "I'd like an answer to my question," he said.

Professor Glass hesitated for a moment and then asked, "Anyone want to take a crack at Jordan's question? Why do people persecute other people?"

Silence. No one wanted to say the wrong thing. No one wanted to upset Jordan.

Donovan, our resident political junky, jumped in.

"In the paper last week there was this article—it was about research done on kids and they followed these kids from when they were young to the age of about twenty-five. When the kids were young, the researchers noted who was insecure and who was secure. The insecure kids grew up to be conservatives and the secure ones grew up to be liberals."

"Hey," said Derek, "I'm a Republican."

"My point exactly," Donovan shot back. The class laughed nervously. We all felt Jordan standing there, still waiting for his answer.

"The point is," he continued, "people want the world to be simple. If you grow up insecure and afraid, you want protection. You want to be able to see who the bad guy is. So you make the world into camps— like gay, bad; abortion, bad; but in other days maybe it was Jews, bad. These guys want the world to be clear cut. That way, it's easy to say certain people are evil and certain people are the cause of all the trouble. Isn't that just what Hitler did, too?"

He stopped. "There are some very screwed up people out there, but they project that onto others and somehow everyone else ends up being the screw-ups in their eyes."

Professor Glass stepped in. "Perhaps what you're trying to say is that truth is an elusive thing. We all think we know the truth. We fight for it, kill for it, die for it. But do we really know the truth?"

Unexpectedly, Jordan spoke up. It was almost as if he were thinking out loud. His voice was quiet but I could hear him. "That's why *The Matrix* was such a big hit. I mean, everyone in that movie thinks they know what's going on. But they don't, do they? I mean it's a totally different reality, but they have no idea."

At first, Jordan talking about some movie struck me as very off, but when I thought about it for a moment, I realized it made perfect sense. Jordan was a science fiction fanatic, for one thing. But more importantly, he was trying to make sense of something that made no sense. He had lived in a world where he couldn't even imagine such a thing happening. Well, welcome to my world. I couldn't have imagined it either—until they came to my door that day with the news about Saul. I couldn't imagine that my basically safe world could be turned upside down in that split second. Just like in *The Matrix* the world I thought was real wasn't real at all.

Donovan picked up where Jordan left off. "If you scare people enough—like in *V for Vendetta*, or like right here, right now, in this country—no one can think straight and you can make them do just about anything."

"And that is very much the history of persecution," Professor Glass said, trying to bring the discussion back to Jordan's question. "Make a group of 'bad guys,' blame them for whatever is wrong in society, and—

back to Donovan's point—the world becomes simple and easy to navigate."

"They're sick." Jordan said. "Sick."

And with that, he turned and left the room.

Again there was a long silence. Professor Glass took a swig of water and sighed. "Let's carry on," she said.

I wondered if I should go after Jordan. I was already at the back of the class, so I decided to just slip out and see if he was still there. When I got outside the hall was empty. I went back in, but it wasn't easy concentrating on the rest of the class.

The discussion turned to the Inquisition and that's when I remembered my dreams. Had I somehow been dreaming what we were studying? If that were the case it would be a relief. These dreams were so vivid and powerful that I was beginning to worry.

Stephanie was describing exactly what the Inquisition was and I needed to pay attention. "Heresy," she was saying. "In 1233, the Roman Catholic Church and Pope Innocent the Third established a tribunal to punish heretics and, of course, to discover who they were. The tribunal first published an 'edict of grace' in whatever town they would descend upon. Heretics were expected to confess immediately; whoever didn't confess could then be accused by the tribunal of heresy under an '*auto-da-fe*,' or 'act of faith.' They could be tortured and imprisoned in dreadful conditions until they did confess. Even if they finally did confess, all their possessions were taken. Many women were property owners then, and some scholars believe this was the Church's way of seizing their property with no penalty. After the Inquisition, the power of women was much diminished."

I vaguely remembered reading a book called *The Burning Time*, which was all about that, when I was in middle school. Stephanie paused at this point for emphasis. "If you were lucky," she said, "you confessed, lost your property, and got to die by strangulation before they burned you. Not so lucky and you were burned alive, after being tortured forever. Nice. Talk about evil."

Just then, Barbara grabbed my wrist. I had been listening so intently that I jumped and almost squealed aloud. "You *need* to believe that evil exists," she said as she stared at me, her voice low and intense. "Otherwise, you can't fight it. You'll be helpless!"

"Okay, Barbara, now you're just freaking me out," I whispered back. I took her hand off my wrist, and noticed she'd left a red mark. I looked over at her and tried to laugh it off. "Very *X Files*."

But Barbara's words and her intensity threw me. It was almost as if she knew something. Did she?

I tried to turn my attention back to Stephanie. She was talking about the Jews now and the Inquisition in Spain. "In the 1400s a man called Tomàs de Torquemada was put in charge of the Inquisition in Spain and basically went crazy. He started to arrest *conversos*—that's what they called the Jews who had converted to Christianity. Torquemada accused them of being secret Jews."

I tried to listen but it was no use. Barbara had totally freaked me out. And seeing Jordan like that had distracted me, too. I felt so badly for him. I still couldn't figure out how his dad and I were connected, or how much danger I was in.

It didn't help that the topic was so gruesome. Finally, after what seemed like forever, the class was over and I hurried to the car. I sat for a minute before driving and thought about what Barbara had said. Evil. Perhaps some sort of possession. Whatever. Maybe it was possible. I'd never really dwelled on any of this— God, evil, suffering. Even after Saul died I just wanted to find out who had done it. All these reasons beyond people just being nuts and cruel had never interested me. Despite Beth's insistence that I consider these matters, it all seemed irrelevant to me. But Barbara and Jordan had made me think. What if there *was* something going on that I couldn't see—not necessarily "spiritual," as Beth would say, but maybe an entire picture I wasn't aware of?

I started the car and headed for the small deli and grocery a few blocks from home. The owner, a wonderful effusive woman from Argentina, Gloria, always had a warm question about the children, and a friendly word about life in general. That day she was all concern and nothing but "tsks" and clucks.

"People," she said, shaking her head. "Why they have to be so bad?"

She wrapped the roasted chicken I'd chosen for dinner and tried to tempt me with some marinated vegetables. "You don't want to cook," she said.

"You're right," I agreed. "Let me have the vegetables and the new potatoes."

She nodded, pleased that I was being so sensible.

"You take it easy now, Ros," she ordered.

"I will, Gloria, I will."

I picked Nate up early and we went to the library on Sunset Drive. We chose five new books as he raced around the room saying, "bu, bu, bu," wanting to pull them all off the shelves and onto the floor. As we headed home with our treasures I tried to behave as if everything was normal. Maybe it all would be again, soon.

I put Nate into his playpen, put away the food, then opened the mail.

"You are next."

The message was on a plain piece of paper, computer typed in bold, and had been mailed to the house.

I felt ill. The blood rushed out of my head, forcing me to sit down. After a moment, I reached for the phone and called Detective Pauls, whose card I'd left beside the phone.

"There's a chance it could just be a prank," he said, after picking up on the first ring. "But we can't take that risk. I'd like to drop over and get it."

If it wasn't a prank then the killer was still very much with us. It *must* be a prank, I thought. It had to be.

I felt frantic. What could I do to protect myself and Nate? I realized that the dial tone was buzzing in my ear and I was frozen in the chair. Slowly I put the phone down, got up, walked over to Nate and picked him up.

"It'll be okay," I said, holding him so tight that he began to wriggle and squirm. "It'll be okay."

6.

Detective Pauls dropped over and picked up the note. He put it in a plastic baggie, said he'd look into it, and was off.

I fed Nate and then we read all the new books one after the other. I watched him totter around the room going from toy to toy, bringing each one to me to share the fun. His newest thrill was a pull-toy dog that barked whenever it moved, but learning to pull it was hard. Nate tried over and over again, determined to get it right.

"Choice," I muttered to myself. "When things are out of your control the only choice you have is how you'll react." Dad always used to say that to me—a lesson he learned from his parents and their experiences in Germany and in the camps, which they somehow survived.

I didn't want to be a victim, but someone was trying to make me one. I needed to do something. It was only around five o'clock. Nate had already eaten and so had I—at least what I could manage. He usually went to sleep early, but maybe tonight could be an exception. We'd go out. It was Thursday, the night of the weekly street fair. I'd put him in his stroller, we'd walk over there, have an ice cream, maybe even stop in at the bookstore and see what was new. I wouldn't stay home and cower. I wouldn't.

I put on my sneakers, snapped Nate into his stroller, and headed down to Palm Canyon Drive. The night was warm and there was a slight breeze. Happy, carefree crowds packed the street, which was cordoned off to traffic. Many of the shops were open, but the main attractions were the booths that lined each side of the road. Everything was for sale—from jewellery, to scented candles, to handbags, to farmers' booths jammed with fresh produce. An entire block was dedicated just to food: pizza, souvlaki, hot dogs, fresh baking, and homemade chocolate fudge. I went straight to my favourite ice cream shop, and although we had to stand in line, it was well worth the wait. I ordered banana and dark chocolate for me and plain vanilla for Nate. I fed Nate first. He was so funny, letting me spoon it into his mouth as he said, "Co, co," for cold, and "mmmm," for yummy. Mine had already started to melt. I ate it as we walked down the street, Nate with his soother—"soo"—in his mouth.

The Starry Skies bookstore is the preferred hangout for writers and university types, students and profs alike. There are always readings of one sort or another going on and you can sit at a table, drink a coffee or tea, and often be pleasantly surprised at what you hear. I decided to go in—a rare treat since I usually spend most nights at home, studying and putting Nate to bed. Besides, I'd certainly be safe there, and might even meet up with someone I knew. Surprised is hardly the word I'd use to describe my reaction when I walked into the main room. There, on the small makeshift stage, reading a poem, was none other than Detective Pauls. I sat down at the back to listen.

"An Unkindness of Ravens," he announced.

"Chihauhuan Ravens surf a vortex of wind
above the city
a silent pledge of change

celebrating flight

because they can and right now
no other desire or need matters more
than being together—flying."

It was good. Not at all what I would have expected
from a hard-boiled detective. Everyone clapped.
"A Theory of Relativity," he said.

"the mouse sitting under the Paloverde
demonstrates its superior perspective:
by being closer to the ground she has
the truer feel of desert sands. Undoubtedly
she could address discrepancies among grains

whereas the Red-tailed Hawk reads patterns
the mouse is innocent of such wider contexts
so she won't notice that it is she who teaches
the hawk how to touch the ground."

More applause.
"Osprey Gliding," he said.

"loud seagull-like screams approach
and the sky reveals an Osprey
gliding above the palms

it won't find fish
in this desert; it must return across the range
or head for the Salton Sea

it issues a challenge as it circles above us,
as if to say, 'don't be surprised by surprises:
nothing is only what it seems.'"

More clapping and then he said, "Thank you," and
went to sit with a group of friends. Just as he reached
their table he noticed me and walked over.

"Mrs. Green," he said, and I could swear he looked
embarrassed. Only then did I realize that he must be
quite a bit younger than I'd initially thought. Maybe
late twenties at the most. His craggy face made him
look older at first glance—plus his height and those
piercing blue eyes. "I hope that reading wasn't too
painful for you."

"Not at all," I smiled. "I liked it very much. And
please, call me Ros."

"Then you should call me Allan."

I nodded. There was an awkward pause. Should I ask
him to join me, I wondered? But no, he was with friends
and was probably just trying to be polite. He hovered
near the table, his fingers drumming on the other chair.

"Nice to see you out," he said.

"I decided to refuse to be bullied," I answered.

"Good," he said. "Do you like poetry?"

"I do," I replied. "A lot."

He nodded.

Another awkward pause.

"Have you been writing long?" I asked.

"Since high school." He smiled then—an act that completely transformed his face. "Everyone writes poetry in high school, right? I just never got over it. And you? You're at school?"

"Just first-year university."

"Do you like it?"

"I do."

He looked at Nate—who was looking around, alert but quiet—and seemed to feel he needed to say something. "He seems a happy boy."

I smiled. "He is. Although it's hard for him, to have only me. My husband was a policeman, you know."

He did. "I read about his case as part of this investigation. I'm very sorry. We're looking into his death as well, just in case there's a connection."

I was surprised. What kind of a connection could there be?

Someone at his table started waving to him. He murmured a quick goodbye and walked back to his friends.

I had a cup of tea while someone else got up and read poetry he'd put to music—kind of Leonard Cohen-ish, but not as good. Soon after, Nate started to get fussy. I paid, nodded goodbye to Allan, and started out the door, only to bump into Maureen.

"Ros!" she exclaimed. "I was just thinking of you!"

"Hi, Maureen," I said, trying not to let my lack of enthusiasm show.

"This must be your darling little boy," she gushed. "Just look at him! Gorgeous! Those long lashes and brown eyes, and that curly hair," she bent down and ruffled Nate's hair, "just like his father. Now, you must let me take you to lunch. We'll go to Marvin's. The food is fabulous! Tomorrow. Tomorrow lunch?"

"I can't," I said quickly. "I don't have daycare for Nate tomorrow."

"You *can't* say no," she insisted. "We'll ask Beth if she'll look after him."

What a lot of nerve, I thought.

"No, I can't," I protested.

"Nonsense. I'll call Beth and arrange the whole thing. I'll pick you up. What's your address? Never mind. I remember."

She barreled past me, calling, "See you then," over her shoulder as she went.

I could have kicked myself. Why had I let her steam-roll over me like that? Well, at least she'd chosen a wonderful restaurant. And maybe she was nicer than she looked . . . or seemed. . . .

7.

The sky goes on and on forever—a deep blue, broken by cumulous clouds that reach miles into the air. The terrain, rolling hills, also seems to go on and on. Suddenly, Father is standing beside me. He looks worried. Terribly worried.

"Rosa, there is something I must tell you," he says. "A terrible secret. But a secret no more."

From out of a cloud a thunderclap sounds. "It's not safe," he says. But I don't think he means the far-off cloud. The wind begins to whip my skirts. The sky turns a terrible colour, green and grey. My skin becomes cold and clammy and I feel hot and cold together.

❧

Again, the vividness of the dream was startling. These were like no dreams I had ever had before. I was dressed in the clothes from my other dream, the dream of burning, and my father was calling me Rosa. As I thought about it, I realized he wasn't speaking English, but Spanish. I speak Spanish fairly well, because I took it in school. Was I dreaming about Spain? I tried to remember what Spain might look like, but I'd only ever seen it in movies or pictures. Still, from what I recalled, the dream terrain certainly could have been Spain. And I'd been studying Spain and the Inquisition, so really it made sense in a way—that I was somehow making up a story about what I'd been studying. Quite a vivid story, though. I'd studied plenty of history before and never had dreams like this. I suppose they were unusual because of the strain I was under. Maybe all the stress around the murder had simply thrown my subconscious something it could only deal with in this way.

When Nate got up, we ate breakfast and then went to the park. He played in the sandbox and on the swings—his favourite. It was a gorgeous day, and we stayed until it was time to go home for Nate's lunch. I fed him, then took him over to Beth's where she put him down for a nap in a portable playpen.

Back home I put on a calf-length black skirt and long-sleeved black twin set. I was ready for Maureen when she picked me up. She was driving a bright red BMW convertible and the roof was down.

Marvin's is a small restaurant, nestled right up against the mountains. The food is wonderful and the service always friendly, never snooty. I ordered salmon, which was delicious and Maureen ordered a seafood pasta dish. She talked almost non-stop; quite a feat, because she ate non-stop, too—soup, salad, main course, and then dessert.

"After high school, I went to L.A. and got my real estate license," she said. "I could've done anything, but I liked the idea of real estate. I don't just buy and sell, you understand," she explained. "I'm a developer, too. You know that huge new project in Palm Desert—The Cornerstone? That's me—or my company. And I'm also partners with a big firm in San Diego."

I nodded and tried to look interested. And wondered how on earth she had managed all this in the few years since we'd graduated.

Just then a man came over to our table to say "hi" to Maureen.

"Well, that's right on cue," she laughed. "Robert, join us a minute. This is an old friend of mine from school, Ros Green. Ros, Robert Mendoza."

We shook hands. He was quite nice looking, dark hair, brown eyes, medium height, wearing casual pants and a grey sweater. Nothing startling, just pleasant the way it was all put together. Oh, and a nice smile.

"Robert is one of my partners in the Palm Desert deal," Maureen explained. A group of young hot shots, I thought. I mean, I was a year younger than all my classmates, but even so, Maureen was only twenty or twenty-one. Here she was with a BMW, business partners, and probably some big flashy house on top of all that. And here *I* was in first year university with not two pennies to rub together. I knew my instinct to say no to lunch had been right. Maureen and I had pretty much nothing in common. Not that I have anything against money, but I want to make the world better somehow—maybe be a teacher or a professor, like my mom and dad.

"Nice to meet you," Robert said, and shook my hand with a firm grasp. His hand was warm and dry. I found myself smiling back.

"Ros was with Dr. Graham when . . ." Maureen's words trailed off, her voice low.

"It was you? Oh, I'm so sorry," he said. "You look well." He paused. "I knew Dr. Graham. We were adversaries, in fact. Friendly adversaries," he assured me.

"Oh?" I said.

"Dr. Graham was a fanatic environmentalist, you know," Robert explained. "He was active in that group,

Earth Matters. They were trying to block our development in Palm Desert. Something about it being a mountain goat habitat." He shook his head. "Slowed us down something terrible."

"Well, I hope you didn't shoot him over it," I blurted out, then immediately felt like an idiot. But he took no offense.

He smiled. "We have lawyers," he answered with a smile. "Who needs guns?"

I smiled back. I couldn't help myself. It wasn't what he said, he was just charming.

He shook my hand again, saying how lovely it had been to meet me, then returned to his own table.

Maureen winked at me. "He likes you," she said. "Quite a catch, too. Rich as hell. And only twenty-five."

"I'm not interested," I said. "I mean, in general."

"Well, you were going out with Dr. Graham."

I looked at her, stunned. "What? He was older than my own dad! What would make you think that? I'm friends with his son, Jordan, who maybe I was sort of going out with, but not really."

"Oh," Maureen paused for a moment, a puzzled look on her face. "I'd heard you two were quite an item."

I was completely flabbergasted.

"From who?"

"Who knows," she shrugged. "It's a small town."

"But that's just too weird," I said. "I can't imagine how that could have gotten around. Someone with a very sick mind."

"It's not that weird," she said. "I liked him myself. We'd been out a couple times since his divorce." The look on my face must have said it all.

"No, nothing like that! To discuss this project, see if we could come to an understanding. I asked him out. Best not to get the lawyers involved, if possible."

She asked me about my classes then, but it was just to be polite. Maureen was far more interested in *me* hearing about *her* than vice versa. She told me that her career had started when she bought a house for $30,000 with money her granddad had left her, and flipped it for $60,000. She used that to buy more, made a million-dollar sale on a condo in Palm Desert, et cetera, et cetera. I ate my food, nodded, smiled, and made noises as if I was impressed.

She did ask me about Nate—how I managed to go to school and look after him, things like that.

"I have to get going," I said, when I finally decided it would no longer be terribly rude. "I need to get my stitches out."

"Who's your doctor?" she asked.

"Strong."

"Not exactly a warm and fuzzy kind of guy," she said.

"What do you know about him?"

"He's one of the leaders of the anti-abortion movement here. He'd probably heard of you and Dr. Graham—your volunteer work at the clinic."

"Well that explains a lot," I mused. I didn't voice the other thought I that was in my head. How did Maureen know all this? She seemed to know everything about everybody.

I had just enough time to get to the hospital. Dr. Strong wasted no more time on me than was absolutely necessary and I was glad to see the last of him. As he walked away, I couldn't help but wonder if he might actually know who shot me. After all, the right-to-lifers did have a pretty tight network, especially the fanatical wing. I remembered the murderer that the police had captured in Europe, and all the people here in the U.S. who had helped him elude the law for so long.

Even if Dr. Strong hated me, he must have done a good job. With the stitches out, I could move my arm pretty freely. I headed for the door, happy to be on my way. As I was leaving the examining room, though, I was suddenly confronted by Dr. Graham's ex-wife.

"I heard you were coming in today," she said. "Do you have a minute?"

"I really don't have a second—never mind a minute—for any more of your accusations," I said, trying unsuccessfully to make my way past.

"You're right," she said. "I was terribly upset at the funeral." She paused. "Just a quick coffee?"

I was more than a little curious. What was so important that she had obviously lain in wait for me?

"All right," I agreed.

I followed her to the cafeteria. She got herself a coffee and I asked for an iced tea. As we sat down I said, "How did you know I would be here?"

"I work here," she said. "That's how my husband and I met. I'm in the administration office—vice-president, in fact."

I nodded, not really knowing what to say. Congratulations? And that still didn't explain how she knew I'd be there, unless she'd gone to some trouble to track me down.

"I'd like to know what kind of relationship you had with Michael," she said, staring directly into my eyes.

"Why?" I asked, immediately wondering if she'd heard the same rumours as Maureen.

"Michael and I had been seeing a lot of each other the month before he died," she stated. "I felt we were on our way to a reconciliation."

"The thing is, I didn't really have a relationship with

your husband," I said. "If I did, it was as his friend. It was more about your son, Jordan. We're in the same Jewish studies class."

She gripped her coffee cup so tightly that her knuckles went white. "This whole thing must somehow be down to you," she blurted out. "Michael had no enemies. He was shot at your house! If it had been an abortion killing he would've been shot at the clinic or at his house. You may come across as Little Miss Innocent, but you obviously have enemies—and you don't make those kind of enemies by being a good little girl. You stole my husband. And as a result, I lost my children's father."

I stood up, trembling from head to foot. "I don't know where this rumour started, but it isn't true! I didn't steal your husband and I won't listen to any more of this."

I grabbed my bag and walked away. I looked back to see her glaring at me with pure hatred in her eyes.

In the parking lot, I sat in my car for a few minutes to collect myself before starting the engine. I took a few deep breaths. She was nuts! And all that venom! Could she have hated her ex-husband enough to kill him? Or had she tried to kill me, killing Dr. Graham by mistake? If it wasn't that, she obviously needed to blame someone. Clearly, I was it.

But what if she *were* right in some way? Why *had* the shooter come to my house? And that note. If they'd been after Dr. Graham, surely it would be over now, but the note seemed to demonstrate that it wasn't over. And who had spread these rumours about me and Dr. Graham. And why?

I needed to pick up Nate—and call that security company.

8.

The weeping woman in the bedroom is my mother. There is a trunk on the floor, open and already half full.

"Mother," I whisper, "where are you going?"

She looks up, wipes away her tears.

"We are all going," she says. "Leaving everything behind. We never should have come. Hatred lives wherever you go."

This did not sound like my mother, the gentlest person in the world.

Suddenly a pounding on the door. My father's voice. Shouts. Mother points to the trunk. I am frozen to the spot and can't move. Boot steps on the stairs.

She grabs me and pushes me into the trunk, slamming the lid. I can hear men entering the room, the heavy footfalls. She

is struggling. And then they are dragging her, "Dear Lord, no,"
she protests, "Don't do this. No."

And then all is quiet.

                                   ✄

"Ros. Ros. Wake up."

Beth was standing over me. I must have fallen asleep on the couch. Nate was down for the night and the book I'd been studying lay open on my chest. "I knocked, but you must have been right out. Chris is actually home, so I thought I'd drop over. I used my key, hope you don't mind. Stay put," she ordered as she headed for the kitchen. "I'll put on the kettle."

She returned with strong tea a few minutes later.

I took a few sips and shook my head, trying to clear it. "I've been having the strangest dreams," I admitted, still very much in the grip of the last one.

"Tell me," she said.

This time I did. I told her about all of them—from the first time in the hospital to the one I'd just had. I explained that they were beginning to really trouble me, that a story seemed to be emerging. But how could that be? Was that normal?

"They are so unlike any dreams I've ever had," I said. "They are so vivid, it's really like I'm there. I mean, it doesn't feel like I'm dreaming at all. The setting seems so familiar and yet I don't think it's anywhere I've actually been. I'm trying to figure out if it's somewhere I've seen in a movie or travelogue or something." I paused and looked down at my book. "I'm thinking it's just some sort of weird dramatization of what I'm studying. You know, the Inquisition," I waved the book. "The *conversos*, stuff like that."

"Hold on, hold on," Beth said. "I may be good at diagnosing spots, and I can definitely tell you if it's diaper rash, measles, or an allergy, but you've lost me on this. Who were the *conversos*?"

"They were Jews in Spain and Portugal who were forced to convert," I explained. "And this was the time of the Inquisition, so they were *really* made to convert."

"Right," said Beth, "or they were tortured and burned. Okay."

"But even if they converted they were often still accused of being secret Jews," I replied, "and I guess some of them did practise in secret. In my latest dream we were speaking Spanish." I tapped the book. "So, it makes sense, right, that I'd be dreaming about all this? I'm just regurgitating what I'm learning in class."

"When did you start studying the Inquisition?"

"We just did."

"Well, then your explanation works," Beth said, "except for one thing."

"What?"

"The first dream you had was in the hospital, right?"

"Right."

"And you started reading about this *after* your last class, and your prof lectured on it when?"

"During the last class."

"So why did you dream about it the day of the shootings?"

I stared at her. There had to be a logical explanation.

"Well," I said slowly, "Professor Glass must have talked about it during her initial overview at the beginning of the year. Maybe the stress just made me focus on it for some reason."

"But for what reason?" Beth said.

I sighed. "Oh, I don't know. Some weird subconscious thing."

Beth looked at me skeptically. "Yes," she agreed. "But what? You need to throw away all your fixed ideas. Maybe the dreams are filled with clues and have nothing to do with the Inquisition at all. Maybe the Inquisition is a symbol for you—a symbol that represents the evil around you, starting with Saul's death and leading up to this. And maybe somewhere in those dreams are names and faces that your subconscious is trying to get you to remember."

"Now that makes sense," I said. "I'm relieved. I thought you were going to come up with something more far out than that."

"Like what?" she smiled. "A past life or something?"

I smiled. "Yes, like that."

"And what if it is?"

I grabbed the pillow from under me and threw it at her.

"You're hopeless!" I said.

"Well, that's true, *but,* dreams this vivid are often really past life memories. If you are reliving one particular life, there has to be a reason for it."

"Come on," was all I could reply.

"Maybe there's a connection between these dreams and Dr. Graham's murder—through symbol or through something more concrete. That's all I'm saying."

"But there's no connection! Nothing. I'm *sure* one thing has nothing to do with the other. Probably all of this stress is causing me to lose my mind. How can I be there for Nate if I'm going nuts?"

"Why assume you're going crazy? Why not assume your brain is a treasure trove of information and your higher mind is trying to help you? I mean, logic can't

explain everything." She shook her head in exasperation and her ponytail whipped back and forth. "Do you
really believe the universe is an orderly little jigsaw
you can just manipulate and that everything will fit
together in the end? And what makes you think that it
will keep you safe to deny something as powerful as
your dreams? You need to open your mind, Ros."

I was starting to get annoyed. Beth was lecturing
me about her weird ideas and theories again. It was
ridiculous to think that these crazy dreams could have
anything to do with Dr. Graham's murder.

"I'm not trying to scare you," Beth continued.
"Hopefully this madness is all over now. I just don't
want you to miss something. It's like you're being
given a gift most people never receive. A clue."

She sounded like a character out of that cheesy
movie, *Serendipity*—all fixated on clues and signs from
the universe. If there is a higher power, why does he,
she, or it need to resort to clues? It just seems so lame.
Of course, Mom and Dad love that movie. I've
watched it with them so many times I can recite the
lines. I put my head in my hands.

"I've never told you how I got into all this stuff,
have I?" Beth asked.

"Not really," I said. And both of us knew why. I was
such a skeptic Beth didn't even want to get started.

Plus thinking about all of this just made me think about Saul—and that was way too painful most of the time.

"I was in med school, living in an old house off campus with five other girls. At night, we'd hear these weird noises, crying and footsteps, and things would move mysteriously. All of us were med students. Different backgrounds, though— Jewish, R.C. like me, two Protestants, and a Muslim. One night, I saw her clear as day. I mean, I thought it was a visitor dressed up for something. A young woman in a fifties-style dress. And then, one by one, we all saw her at different times. So we decided to look up the history of the house and there it was—a young student had died there, but no one ever discovered the how or why. It appeared that she just stopped breathing in her sleep, but her friends always suspected her jealous boyfriend of suffocating her." Beth paused. "And then I had some even stranger experiences with people I was looking after in the ER. People who had near-death experiences. It was something you couldn't ignore."

A knock at the door startled both of us. I'd been listening so intently that I jumped at the sound. "More another day," Beth said as she got up to answer the door. She returned with Susana, who had a load of clothes thrown over her arm.

"I don't want to hear the word 'no' come out of your mouth," she announced as she strode into the living room. "These clothes are not selling, so I'm marking them down to 60 percent off, 75 percent for you." She threw a silk pair of cream-coloured pants and a long peaches-and-cream silk top onto the couch. She added a black pair of pants, a black and white top, and a very cool pair of jeans to the pile.

"I can't!" I exclaimed. "These must be worth a fortune."

"I'm telling you, it's old stock," Susana said. "Now just go try it all on."

"Look at you," she crooned, as I emerged from my bedroom in the silk outfit. "It's perfect."

I forced myself to smile instead of cry. I was so touched I was very tempted to do the latter. "You are way too soft," I chided. "How are you going to make a living if you carry on this way?"

"I'm telling you," she repeated, "this was all going on sale anyway. Not too many people around with your height and build." She paused. "You know, like Amazons."

Beth poured her a cup of tea, and we sat around and chatted for awhile almost like everything was normal.

"Oh, I almost forgot," Susana said scrabbling around in her purse. She drew out a DVD set and held it up.

"Season Four of *Curb Your Enthusiasm*. Thought you could use a few chuckles."

We decided to watch the first episode together. I made popcorn. And we laughed our heads off. That poor schmo—he could never get anything right.

9.

The next morning was Moms and Ones at the library and I didn't want to miss it. Beth and I always go together. Nate kept plopping himself in the teacher's lap as she read the books at the end of the class, but she didn't mind. And he had his first chocolate— M&Ms no less. I'd resisted until then but somehow all my little rules suddenly seemed overdone. How could a little chocolate hurt? He couldn't get enough of them. The other moms were all very sympathetic about the shooting, but no one dwelled on it, which was good. It's a great group, and such a relief to talk non-stop about teething, ear infections, and what to do when your precious is throwing a tantrum. Just knowing that other moms are going through the same things as you with their kids is priceless.

We took Highway 111 on the way back, and I was anxious to get home. The security firm was coming that afternoon and I wanted to get Nate down for his nap before they arrived. Beth and I were chatting about one of the moms, Corrine, who had a terrible temper and yelled at her daughter all the time. We were trying to figure out what we could say to her next time to help her cope and save poor Brenna from a traumatic childhood. A siren interrupted our conversation. I looked in my mirror as I pulled over. A fire engine was coming up fast behind us. As it roared past us I saw that it wasn't alone—it was followed by a second truck and an EMS vehicle. Whatever had happened, it was serious. All three vehicles turned right on Sunshine Way, the same cut-off we had to take to get home. The light turned red before we could turn, however, and I needed to wait. Traffic was sparse so when we finally did turn I saw the flashing red lights slow a little at an intersection up ahead. Beth was beside me, the kids in the back in their car seats.

"Beth?" I said.

She knew what I was thinking.

My throat went suddenly dry and my heart began to pound in my chest.

"Don't be silly," Beth said. "What are the chances it's one of our places?"

And then the trucks turned. I was at least a couple blocks behind them but it looked like they might have turned onto Mesa Road. Our street.

I followed. I think I was muttering something like, "no, no, no," but I'm not sure. Then I was driving down our street, and everything seemed to slow down and speed up all at the same time.

The trucks were in front of my house. Smoke was pouring out of the windows.

I pulled in just behind the trucks.

"Stay with the kids, please," I said to Beth.

"That's my house," I shouted to the firefighters as I flung myself out of the car. "That's my house."

"Just stay back," one said. "Is there anyone at home?"

"No, there's just me and my son." I pointed to the car.

"Well, that's a good thing," the man replied, and left me to do his job.

"I'm so sorry."

I whirled around to see Allan Pauls.

"What are you doing here?" I asked him.

"I left a standing order that if anything to do with your case comes up, I'm to be notified," he said. "This came over the radio a few minutes ago and I was just down at the station. Lucky you were out."

"I must have left something on. The stove, maybe."

"Maybe," he said. "But we need to consider that it might be arson."

"Arson?"

"It wouldn't be the first time someone tried to hurt you."

"But I wasn't home!"

"Maybe they didn't want to hurt you in that way—maybe they just wanted to make you suffer."

"But why?" I almost wailed.

Just then the fire chief came up to him.

"Detective?"

"Lorimer, right?" Allan said.

"Right. There was almost definitely an accelerant used in this fire. It's pretty much under control now, but it'll be a while before it's safe to go in."

So Allan had been right. Was that some kind of gut instinct police had? Someone had tried to burn my house down.

"I need to call my parents," I said.

"Maybe you should wait," Allan said quietly.

"What?"

"Maybe it's better if they aren't around. You and your family are in danger right now," he said. "In fact, perhaps you should go and join them until we have this straightened out."

I didn't know what to do or what to think or where to turn. "My brother lives in Vancouver. That would be a lot easier than going to Australia," I said. Although I didn't want to say it, it would be a lot cheaper, too. "But what about school? Exams are coming up. I don't want to lose my year."

"Look, Ros, I'm sorry, but your house, the shooting, the note. I'd have to say you and Nate are in danger."

"But why?" I exclaimed again. "I don't have enemies. I mean, why?"

"We're going to have to think on that," he said. "In the meantime, can you check into a hotel for tonight? I can take you."

I nodded. I couldn't think. I couldn't feel. I couldn't understand.

10.

I am standing in a large room. The ceilings are high. On a dais in front of me are three men, all dressed in black. They sit behind a large imposing wooden desk. The middle-aged man in the centre has a long white face. His eyes are cold. On one side of him a plump older man sits, folding and unfolding his hands. On the other side is a very young man, strikingly handsome.

"You are a Jewess," the man in the middle says, his voice booming. He speaks in Spanish.

"I am not!" I reply.

"You must confess or suffer the consequences. You will tell us the truth."

"I swear to you," I cry, "I am not. I was raised a good Catholic. I know nothing of this other faith. Even under torture I will not be able to tell you what you want to know."

"Oh, you will tell us," the voice booms. "But first you will watch your father and mother burn. Take her."

Suddenly, I am in a square and there are two people tied to a stake set into the middle of a wooden platform. Underneath the platform is kindling wood. My dearest father and mother.

"Don't make the child watch," my mother pleads.

And then, as the fire is lit and creeps up on them, I hear my father. He is speaking in a strange tongue. He is calling out in it. But I don't know what it means.

⌇

I sat up in bed, the words of the dream still echoing in my mind. I didn't understand them in the dream, but I remembered them completely when I awoke.

"Shema Israel, Adonai Elohanu, Adonai Ehad."

"Here O Israel, The Lord is our God, The Lord is One."

The words all Jews say when they are in prayer—the prayer they are most likely to say when they are dying.

I looked at the clock. It was eight-thirty. I'd slept in and miraculously so had Nate. He was sitting up now in his portable playpen, chatting happily to his tiger. We were at a small motel on Highway 111, run by this really sweet gay couple. Mom and Dad always have friends coming to the desert to visit, and since we don't have a guest room, they put them up here. Each room is decorated like a little individual home with a four-poster bed, flowers on the wallpaper, a small kitchen, and a table that looks out onto the courtyard. The courtyard is full of flowers and cactus and there's a pool, of course. In the morning, there's breakfast served beside the office. I took advantage of Nate's good mood to jump in the shower and then put on the same clothes from yesterday. I dressed Nate, who'd slept in his T-shirt, and we went for breakfast.

Lester immediately started fussing over me. He put Nate in a high chair and brought him fruit, already cut into tiny little pieces. For me, there was strong tea, a warm muffin, and some cereal and milk. Surprisingly I ate everything he put in front of me. In fact, I was starving.

Lester had already called the insurance agent for me—his was the same as Mom and Dad's because he'd recommended the firm to them in the first place—and I was supposed to meet them at the house at eleven for a preliminary assessment. And to talk about a cheque I could use right away for necessities.

I called the police and the fire department and was told that it was all right for me to visit the house, they had all the forensic evidence they needed. Lester ordered a cab and Nate and I got to the house at around ten-thirty. It looked dreadful from the outside, blackened with smoke, windows broken.

I knocked on Beth's door. "Are you all right?" she asked, taking my hand. "I wasn't sure where you'd gone."

"I'm sorry. We ended up at The Rose Gardens. I know you wanted us to stay with you," I said, stopping her before she had a chance to lecture me, "but I was so stunned I didn't really know what was happening and Detective Pauls said 'hotel' and when we got in the car I thought of Lester."

"You're forgiven," Beth said. "Let me see if Cynthia can watch the babies. Then I'll go through the house with you."

"Would you?" I said, incredibly relieved. "That would be good. I'm not sure I can manage on my own."

Soon, Nate and Lisa were playing together happily, under Cynthia's watchful eye. Cynthia is a single older woman who lives across the street. We secretly call her Mrs. Santa. Not only does she look just like Mrs. Claus—middle-aged, pleasantly plump, rosy cheeked—but each Christmas she puts up a magnificent display that people from all over the city come to see.

"Come on," Beth said. "Let's get it over with."

Police tape surrounded the house, but there was no sign of any officers.

"How did it happen?" Beth asked as we walked toward the front door.

"Arson."

I ducked under the yellow tape and we walked in the front door. The beautiful cozy home I'd grown up in was in ruins, just like my life. *Why* kept screaming in my head. Why? Why? Why?

The walls were almost black, the tile on the floor also blackened, the floors still soggy with water. But Beth seemed surprised.

"It's not half as bad as I thought it would be," she said. "I'm no expert, but the structure seems all right."

"It's because they got here so fast, at least that's what the fireman told me this morning when I called," I said. "Another five minutes and the whole house would've been a write-off, but it's all inside damage, fire and water."

"That's good," Beth said, trying to sound upbeat.

"I guess," I said as I looked around. I headed for the hutch behind the dining room table and opened it. Oddly enough everything inside was almost untouched. The family pictures, including all the new ones of Nate and the old ones of me and Saul were fine, even our wedding photos. When I saw that I started to cry. Beth held onto me until the worst of the fit was over. Then, with me clutching my wedding album to my chest, we went to look at the rest.

The kitchen looked pretty bad.

"You have to get away from here," Beth said as we walked carefully down the hall. "Someone is out to hurt you in the worst way."

I nodded. "Can I call my brother from your house? I'll get on a flight tonight."

Gingerly I stepped into my bedroom. It wasn't too bad.

"I'll go get a bag," said Beth. "You can collect the jewellery and the pictures and leave them all at my house if you want."

She was back soon, but even the few minutes alone in that house made me feel vulnerable—as if the maniac who had done all of this was somewhere nearby, just trying to figure out what to do next.

I put the jewellery in one bag and then collected the photos and other things from the living room. Miraculously some of my grandmother's china, plates, and figurines on the hutch were untouched. Then we went into my parents' room where books were lined floor to ceiling on shelves including the walk in closet that was used as a small library.

I thought my heart would break at the sight. Mom and Dad and I loved to read—loved books of all kinds. We had thousands of them, and now they were all covered in water.

"We may be able to save quite a few of them."

I whirled around.

A neatly dressed young woman stood behind me. She had light brown hair cut straight at her shoulders, bangs, and pale lipstick. She wore a beige summer suit and low beige heels. She was the picture of good taste and exuded calm efficiency. She held her slim hand out toward mine. "Martha Russell," she said.

"Thank you so much for getting out here so fast," I said.

"Well, we're here to help," she said. "I'm sorry for your loss. And with your parents away this must be terribly hard for you."

As soon as she said that I started to tear up again. I felt like a little kid. How was I going to cope without them?

"We'll have you back in this house in no time," she assured me.

"Really? How long do you think?"

"Within a month. I've spoken to the fire department, and though we'll have our own engineer go through the house, they think the structure is sound. So it means scraping, cleaning, redecorating—and we can get a company that specializes in saving books. You'll have to pay for their services, though, or we can write you a cheque for replacement cost. . . ."

Martha launched into our various options, but I was having trouble focusing on her words. I needed Mom and Dad to make these decisions and Detective Pauls didn't even want me to tell them about the fire until I was safely out of the city.

I explained this to Martha. She just nodded and said that she would get me sorted out so that I could at least buy clothes and food, even stay in a hotel if we needed to.

"Why don't you both come over to my house," Beth said, "and you can figure the rest of this out there."

When Martha had gone, leaving me with a cheque to tide us over, I called Jon. Being my older brother and self-appointed protector, he almost had a fit when I told him what was going on. I promised him I'd get on the next plane, but when I called the airport there were no seats available until the next day—too many tourists returning home. I could have cried. The next morning seemed like forever away, and I just wanted to get Nate to safety as fast as I could.

11.

Susana called Beth's house looking for me, having read about the fire in the morning paper. Delighted to have found me, she insisted that Nate and I stay with her. She has a lovely two-bedroom apartment on Ramon Way. And there's tight security— -a doorman on at all times. I agreed. At least we could feel safe until the flight in the morning. Beth offered Lisa's portable playpen for Nate to sleep in and we were all set.

"In the meantime, why don't you drive over here," Susana said. "I'll take the day off and go shopping with you. Come on. You'll need a few things just to get by."

"She wants me to go shopping with her," I said to Beth.

"Tell her after lunch," Beth suggested, "and I'll watch the kidlets."

Beth fed me a huge turkey sandwich and soup, and we fed the children at the same time.

"Any more dreams?" she asked.

"Yes."

"Tell me."

I was hardly in the mood for any more theories, but I figured it would take less time to tell her than to fight. I described the latest dream, and repeated that I thought it was just an old history lesson resurfacing.

"You're dreaming about a specific time in history," Beth countered. "There must be a reason."

The doorbell rang then and interrupted our conversation. When Beth returned to the kitchen, Detective Pauls was with her.

"I've been looking for you," he said. "I thought I'd try your neighbour and here you are."

"They don't call you a detective for nothing," I said. I meant it to be a joke but my tone sounded so serious I think it came out more as a snide comment. He had the good grace to ignore it.

"I can't quite figure it," he said. "You don't seem the type to attract enemies."

"Detective Pauls, would you like a cup of coffee?" Beth offered.

"No, thank you," he said before he turned his attention back to me. "I've been at the computer all morning looking at your husband's file. I need to cover all my bases, so I've also asked the university for all of your class lists. We're running them now to see if any bad guys jump out at us."

Beth had been busying herself at the counter, washing dishes and putting away leftover food from lunch. Now she gave me a sly look. "Detective Pauls," she said sweetly, "what do you think of dreams?"

"Allan," he corrected her. "And what do you mean?"

"Typical detective, answering one question with another," she chided. "Do you think they—dreams—mean anything?"

"Certainly," he replied.

"Certainly?" Beth raised her eyebrows and gave me a meaningful look.

"Of course they do," he continued. "Our unconscious speaks to us through our dreams. We have to pay attention."

"Ros tells me you're a poet," she said. "No wonder you're more open to the idea than *some* people."

"It's a pretty standard viewpoint," he replied, shrugging off the comment. "Why are you asking?"

"Ros started having strange dreams right after the shooting," she replied. "And now . . . well, now they're constant. I think they're important, I'm just not sure how." She paused. "It does occur to me that she could be reliving some past life."

Great. Now Allan would think my best friend was a flake. Maybe he'd think I was, too. I rested my forehead in my hand and sighed loudly, hoping he would pick up on my exasperation.

"Well, half the planet believes in reincarnation and maybe they're right," he said. I raised my head and stared at him. Was he joking? He didn't seem to be. "I mean, have you read about children who can take their parents to the old homes where the parents grew up and know everything about the parents and the people living there? Or what about the ones who spontaneously start speaking a foreign language before they're two? Makes you think.

"Tell me about your dreams," he said, looking at me now. "If you want to, that is. It's not a police order or anything, but there might be something there that could help me. Some sort of clue."

Over at the counter, Beth made an "I told you so" face. I resisted the urge to stick out my tongue.

I tried to describe the dreams as briefly as possible. "They seem to be centred somewhere in Spain at the time of the Spanish Inquisition."

Quickly, I told him the story as it was developing.

When I was done he thought for a moment, then said, "I've certainly read about *conversos*. It's fascinating stuff. You know, after hearing you describe these dreams I'd have to agree with Beth."

"Hah!" she exclaimed.

"I'd pay attention to them," Allan continued. "Maybe your subconscious is desperately trying to tell you something. And don't worry. I'll be doing real, scientific police work. I won't be consulting crystal balls." He smiled at me then—a nice, reassuring smile that crinkled the corners of those blue, blue eyes.

"Glad to hear it," I said, trying to smile back. Still, I felt pretty weirded out by what he'd said. I'd expected him to treat the whole thing as a joke—and to get Beth off my case once and for all. Instead, he was almost agreeing with her. I was starting to regret ever confiding in Beth. Now these stupid dreams were taking our focus off the real problem— a very real crazy person out there, somewhere.

Just after Allan left the phone rang again. This time it was Maureen, looking for me. I shook my head and Beth said I was unavailable. There were lots of "uh huhs" and "yeses," and when she finally hung up, she told me that Maureen's friend Robert had offered me a house for a month or so, until mine could be fixed up. I was supposed to call her.

"Maureen is suddenly my best friend," I said to Beth with a grimace.

"I think she just loves to be at the centre of everything," Beth commented. "You're probably the most excitement she's had in ages!"

I decided to call her back and get it over with. And who knew—maybe the offer of the house would come in handy.

"Ros, I can't tell you!" Maureen started as soon as she heard my voice. "When I read the paper I almost died. And my friend, Robert, he remembered you right away. We were talking about it, of course—who isn't? The whole city is talking about it: first the shooting, then your house, why someone very sick is out there. Anyway, Robert has this model home. It's all furnished, just gorgeous, out in La Quinta. He wants you to call him. Do you have a pen?"

"Pen?" I asked Beth. She scrambled around for a pencil and piece of paper. "Okay."

Maureen gave me Robert's number. "Call him!"

"Maybe."

"No maybes! Now how can I get hold of you? Where are you staying?"

"At The Rose Gardens last night."

"Not with a friend? That's crazy. If you don't want to take Robert up on his offer you must come and stay with me. I have a huge house in Thunderbird Villas . . ."

"No, no," I interrupted her. "Susana has offered. We'll stay with her for a bit."

"Good. You shouldn't be alone. Now here's my cell number. You call me if you need *anything*. Is that clear?"

"Yes, Maureen," I said, exhausted. Even two minutes on the phone with her was too much. "That's clear."

"Excellent," she said, and hung up.

I shook my head. "She never even asked how I was."

"People like her aren't interested in how other people are," Beth said. "She wants you to make her life more interesting. What's this other number?"

I told her.

"You're better off with Susana," Beth said. "You don't want to be off in La Quinta in a model home. How much more isolated could you get? And you don't want anyone to know where you're going tomorrow either," she warned me.

"I'll just call him and thank him then," I said. "Who knows? Maybe when I come back from Vancouver it'll be useful."

But when I called Robert, something unexpected happened. Before I knew it, I'd agreed to let him take me and Nate to The Lodge for dinner. Honestly, I don't know how it happened. He was just so nice and friendly and *normal*-sounding, and I guess I was craving normal. Beth told me off; she had already planned to feed us that night and I hardly knew him and what was I thinking. Part of me agreed. I wasn't thinking straight at all. But I really doubted that Robert was going to attack us at one of the fanciest restaurants in the valley. With Beth's big-sister scolding still ringing in my ears I scuttled out of there and drove over to Susana's shop. She left the store in the hands of her assistant and we headed for El Paseo. We shopped. I bought a good pair of pants, a silk top, a pair of shoes, and a jacket for the evening. "That beautiful outfit you brought over," I said to Susana, "is ashes now."

"Never mind. There's more where that came from."

We stopped in at the mall—underwear, bras, night-gowns and T-shirts, clothes for Nate—and then went back to Susana's shop. She pressed two pairs of jeans on me, two fancy T-shirts, and a warm sweater. We arranged that I would move to her apartment that night after dinner, and she gave me a key.

Robert picked Nate and me up from Beth's around five and we had a pleasant drive to The Lodge. The hotel is situated on a hilltop and the dining room looks out over the city. It's a beautiful setting and I found myself relaxing in spite of everything. Nate sat in a high chair and ate his favourite, cut up grapes. He had his sippy cup and some crayons and paper. He was happy.

When dinner came, Nate shared my roast chicken and vegetables and had his craisins for desert. I ate an entire piece of chocolate cake. Robert was amazingly nice. He kept the conversation on safe topics like computers and sports and school and we compared our times at different schools in the cities—he's from La Quinta. It was very relaxed. Just as we were about to leave, my cell rang.

"This is Detective Pauls."

There was something off about his voice. It was so . . . formal. A chill ran down my spine.

"Ros," he said and then paused.

"Yes."

"Look, I have some bad news."

I almost laughed. What else could possibly happen? "What?"

"Where are you? Is Nate with you?"

"Yes. We just finished dinner at The Lodge."

"Can you take Nate to Beth's?"

"Yes," I said slowly. "But we were just on our way to Susana's apartment. We're staying there tonight."

"You'll want to go to the hospital."

"Why?" I whispered, clutching the phone so hard my hand hurt.

"It's Susana. She's been hurt."

"No, I just left her," I said.

"I guess this was just after you left," he said, his voice flat. "Later, when she got into her car, it exploded."

"What?"

"Some kind of very crude fire bomb. She's badly burned."

12.

The words stuck in my throat. For a moment, no sound at all would come out.

"How badly?"

"We don't know yet."

"No," I whispered. "No."

"I'm sorry," he said.

"I can't take Nate to Beth's!" I said. "I can't! Someone is watching me. I can't put any of my friends in danger."

"Then take Nate with you to the hospital. She's at the Eisenhower Center. You won't be able to stay long. I don't even know if she can have visitors."

"Has her family been called?"

"Yes. Look, go back to The Rose Gardens. I'm sure you'll be safe there. Is your flight first thing in the morning?"

"Yes."

"I'm sorry."

I hung up the phone. For a minute, I just stared at Robert, unsure of what to do next.

"Can you drive me to the hospital?"

"Of course," he said, concern written all over his face.

When I told him what Detective Pauls had told me he was shocked. "That doesn't happen in Palm Springs," he said. Just what I'd thought. But I was wrong. Somehow, I was the catalyst. I'd brought this with me, all the way from Los Angeles.

We were at the hospital within fifteen minutes, the drive there silent. I thanked Robert, lifted a sleeping Nate out of the car in his seat, lugged it into the foyer, and struggled over to the information booth.

Susana was in intensive care, waiting to be moved into a special burn unit. I found her mother and father waiting in the hall. I hadn't seen them in years, and couldn't have imagined a worse scenario for a reunion. I put Nate's seat on the floor. Miraculously he was still asleep.

"How is she?" I asked.

"Ros," Susana's mom breathed. "She's burned one of her legs and one of her arms. She has no hair left on her body. It's all burned off." She began to cry. "And one of her ears. . . ."

Susana's father, a vigorous seventy-year-old with a full head of white hair and a creased face, filled the awkward pause. "But her neck is all right. And her face. And her chest. Somehow she managed to throw herself out of the car and roll. The café next door called 911 right away. The ambulance was there within minutes."

"Have you seen her?"

"For a minute. They don't want any visitors now. Paulo should be here soon."

Paulo was Susana's younger brother.

"Ros, I don't understand," Susana's mom said. "The police said this may have something to do with you."

"Someone seems to be trying to hurt the people close to me," I said, no longer able to stop myself from crying. "I'm so sorry."

"Is this your boy?" she asked, looking down at Nate.

"Yes."

"He's beautiful," she raised her eyes and stared blankly down the hall. "You should go home. Nothing to do here."

I nodded. They must hate me, I thought. I hated myself.

I went outside to call a cab and found Robert still waiting. He drove us to the motel and made sure I was settled. I barely remembered saying goodbye.

∽

Fire. Fire everywhere. The smell of burning flesh. A priest is pouring boiling water into a pail. He tells me to remove my stockings. He grabs me and pulls me over to the pail. Another one helps him. They lift my leg and shove it in. The pain is beyond anything imaginable. I scream in agony and utter terror.

"Who else is a secret Jew?"

"No one!"

"Tell us!"

They lift my other leg.

"Wait!" I try to think. Who do I know? "Carmelita." I hate her. She never has a nice word for me. She caused trouble for my parents.

"Carmelita Mattias!" I scream.

"Ah," one of them says. "Now the truth. Who else?"

"No one else."

They raise my other leg again.

"Maria," I shout. Maria is old anyway, I think. Who else? Who else? I can't think of any names.

"Juanita Mozales," I say.

"Who else, who else?"

"I don't know! I don't know!"

They hold my second leg over the boiling water. I shriek, "I'll tell, I'll tell." The names come spilling out. My parents — even though they've already been murdered—my relatives, my friends . . . anything to stop them. Anything. But they plunge my foot into the bucket anyway, and the pain is beyond what I can bear. I scream. And I scream. And I scream.

༄

I sat up in bed crying. It was dark and the digital clock on the bedside table read 4 a.m. The pain from the dream still felt so real. I'd always thought that being burnt would be the worst kind of cruelty, and now, I was dreaming about it. Even worse, it had happened to Susana—because of me.

This had to stop. I had to figure out who was responsible. I went to sit at the table by the window and drew the drapes ever so slightly aside. The palms and the desert willows were silhouetted against the night sky.

Was it a stranger, one of the anti-abortion nuts? Or was it someone I knew?

The dreams were useless! They weren't telling me anything. But then why was I having them? They were so real, and they were creating a story. How bizarre was that? Maybe it *was* time for me to admit that the dreams might be a clue—a window into what was happening. I thought back to the reading I'd done for class.

Something like thirteen thousand *conversos* were put on trial in Spain. That was a huge number of people. And out of that, over fourteen hundred were burned. Was I paying now for an event that happened that long ago? Was it karma or something?

I'd studied reincarnation beliefs in a comparative religion course in high school. As I remembered it, karma means action. It means that *our* actions create strings of other actions, and we have to burn those strings away before our karma is clear. It was something like that anyway. It certainly wasn't about punishment.

I thought about a conversation my parents and I had had at dinner one night, after I'd moved home with Nate. Mom had made some crack about the great shopping karma she'd had that day. I said that I hardly thought karma applied to shopping. Dad wasn't so sure. He said that all religions had different streams within them, so who knew? We were joking, of course. But the whole topic got me thinking about Saul and his death and I said that I didn't—couldn't—believe there was a God watching over us. Dad said it depended on how you saw God. He or She didn't have to be a figure looking down on us all. It could be more of a Creator. Like in Native American lore, I'd said. He'd agreed. "Maybe God is an intelligence," he'd said. "Or a power like creativity. After all, isn't creativity the engine that keeps the world growing?"

"I think it's more an imaginative power," Mom chipped in, "and that bad things happen when people can't imagine. Who could hurt another person if they could actually imagine how that person would feel when hurt? Empathy is our greatest attribute. And maybe it's God's, too. But God can't interfere or we'd have no free will."

"Free will, free will," I said. "That's the answer we'd always get at Hebrew school when one of us asked how God could let the Holocaust happen. God didn't do it, man did it. It's lame."

"Why is it lame?" Dad demanded.

"*If* God made the world, *if* He created us, let Him— or Her—make better ground rules! Rules where sadists don't gun down your husband, for instance."

"I think we all choose what will happen to us before we are born," Mom said, surprising me. I'd never heard her say anything like that before. "We return again and again to learn lessons, and we choose the people we return with. You'll be with Saul again in another life and on the other side, I'm sure you will." She must have noticed that I was staring at her with my jaw open. "You weren't the only one who had to think a lot about God after Saul died, you know," she said. "We loved him, too. I started to read. Life-after-death books, stories about people who had had near-death experiences, all that stuff. Even a book on reincarnation by a Jewish psychiatrist."

I was flabbergasted. Mom had never even hinted that she'd been thinking about this stuff.

But something she said really bothered me. "Are you saying Saul came into this life knowing he was going to be murdered?" I asked. "Because it sure sounds that way. Did six million Jews decide to die?"

"I think it's more that we choose who our parents will be so we can learn certain lessons. Maybe we even choose who we'll marry. You know how Grandma always says things are *beshert*—meant to be? Within certain parameters, I think there are things we *can't* control. The world does run on free choice, after all, and people will make certain choices that can help our hopes for a certain kind of life or crush them. If the latter happens, maybe we have to come back and do it again. I think it's a complicated mix between fate and free will."

I thought about borrowing that book on reincarnation, but I decided I didn't want to think about Saul any more than I had to—which seemed to be every minute anyway. Looking back, I guess it wouldn't have made anything worse. And maybe I would even have learned something. I rubbed my eyes and looked out into the night. When I got to Vancouver and could catch my breath I'd go to the library and see what I could find. In the meantime, I had the dreams to think about.

They were centred on fire, which I had to admit seemed to match the events of my life. Maybe the dreams were clairvoyant in some way, warning me. Or were they actually some other life I'd lived? But if that was the case it almost seemed that I was being punished for something that wasn't even my fault, something that happened hundreds of years ago. I had been *tortured* after all. I wasn't the one who'd betrayed my community—at least not willingly. So how much sense did the punishment angle make? Did karma mean you would suffer for actions taken under duress? That seemed pretty harsh. I mean, we all do so many stupid things in life. If karma really is some kind of punishment, we'd be doomed to spend our lives either making stupid choices or making up for stupid choices. That would be a pretty depressing way to look at life. It just didn't feel right. I could still vaguely remember how much joy my life used to have. And in some ways, like with Nate, it still does. Joy feels so much more natural than hate and guilt and misery. On the other hand, if my experiences over the last little while were to be believed, maybe life was just one big miserable, pointless exercise. At that moment I felt a horrible darkness close in around me. Suddenly, I could understand why some people chose to end it all. If they felt the way I was feeling now all of the time, how could they keep living? I stared into the dark night sky and realized that was exactly where I was—in the dark, lost, and with no way out.

13.

¶ tossed and turned for the rest of the night and woke early. I showered and dressed and was ready for Nate when he opened his eyes. A knock at the door put my heart in my throat, but it was only Allan. Somewhere in the back of my mind, it registered how glad I was to see him. No matter how insane everything around me was, he seemed like a rock. A good solid guy that I was beginning to trust. He came in and sat with me at the table while I fed Nate.

"Do you have a ride to the airport?" he asked.

I shook my head.

"I'll take you."

I fussed over Nate, not wanting to ask the question that had been on my mind all night. I was afraid of what he would say next. If Susana was dead, I didn't think I could bear it.

"I've checked on Susana," he said, as if he could read my thoughts.

I held my breath.

"They're pretty sure she'll be okay. But if she hadn't been so quick-witted. . . . The burns to her leg are the worst. And to her right ear. The rest will heal without surgery. But because of her leg, they say she'll be in the hospital for a while."

I shook my head. "It's my fault."

"How?"

"I don't know."

"Where were you last night when I called?"

"Robert Mendoza took me and Nate out for dinner."

"Robert Mendoza? The developer?"

"Yes."

"How do you know him?"

"Maureen Daly, an old friend—well, someone I know from high school—introduced us. Why?"

"He's part of our investigation of Dr. Graham's death."

"What? Why didn't you tell me? He's been very nice. He even offered me a house to stay in."

"Maybe that's what the killer wants," Allan said, echoing Beth. "To isolate you. Make you an easy target."

"I *am* an easy target! Why not just shoot me? I'm easy to find."

"This person seems to want you to suffer first." He paused. "I'm beginning to think that once you survived the first shooting, the killer realized he or she could make you suffer in other ways. Ways worse than killing you."

I shuddered.

"Robert Mendoza and Dr. Graham had quite a feud going," he said.

"I know, Robert told me. But he said lawyers were always more effective than guns."

Allan nodded. "He has millions sunk into this project—everything, in fact. His whole business. The delays Dr. Graham was responsible for could have put him into bankruptcy."

"But what has that got to do with me?" I said. "I can see him as a suspect for Dr. Graham but...."

"You're right," he said. "Unless these are two different crimes.... Maybe someone who hates you saw you get hurt, and somehow the taboo of doing something bad was removed, they felt freer to act." He took a piece of paper from his pocket—the class lists that the school had provided.

"Dow, dow," Nate insisted. I took him out of his high chair and put him on the floor. I turned on the television and tuned it to the children's channel. Normally I wouldn't use it as a babysitter, but I figured this was a pretty decent exception.

"Not one of my fellow students?"

"I'm just checking. Most of them seem pretty tame. But this woman, Barbara Phillips. She's an avid pro-lifer."

I nodded. "Doesn't surprise me."

"And this Margaret Dove has a criminal record."

I knew whom he meant, but I liked Margaret. She seemed tough, but she was pulling herself out of a pretty bad scene.

"This one worries me most," he said, poking at the page with his finger. "George Fields."

I wracked my brain. "Oh yes. Big guy, sits at the back of religion class, never says anything."

"He's a neo-Nazi."

"Then why is he taking Jewish history?"

"Checking out the enemy."

"That's horrible!"

"We're talking to him today." He folded the list and tucked it back into his pocket. "Let me just make sure your flight is leaving on time."

Allan looked at my flight number and, pulling out his phone, got the airline's number, and placed a call. What I heard next made me very nervous.

"Are you sure? Nothing?" he said. He snapped his phone closed and grimaced.

"I'm really sorry, Ros," he said. "Vancouver is socked in. No planes going in or out. They think the earliest will be this afternoon."

I tried to fight it—the last thing I wanted to was lose it in front of him—but I could feel my face start to crumple. I just needed to get Nate away.

"Look," he said, obviously taking pity on me, "just tell me if I'm off base here." He paused a minute as if deciding if he should go ahead. "I have a place out in A Thousand Palms—a couple acres, three horses, two dogs. Come out there. Have lunch. Ride the horses. Maybe you can fly out this afternoon. In the meantime, I don't think our killer would want to mess with me and the dogs."

"What kind of dogs?" I asked, not knowing at first how to answer.

"German shepherds. Trained, of course."

"All right," I agreed. The offer had taken me by surprise, but I was grateful. Anything to keep Nate safe.

We checked out to the fussing of Lester, who wouldn't let me pay. He'd settle up with my parents, he said, as soon as they got home. Once we were in the car, our conversation turned back to the investigation.

"My partner is doing checks today on all the people from your classes."

"Your partner?"

"Yeah. He was up in L.A. on a special assignment. Just got back today," Allan said. "That's a good thing, too. Need some help on this one, that's for sure."

The drive took about half an hour from the motel. We went down Date Palm so we could stop at the local coffee shop and get some much needed caffeine—me a ginger tea and Allan a triple non-fat latte. We also picked up a few cranberry muffins, pieces of which I fed to Nate, twisting around in my seat to pass them back each time he asked for "more."

The flowers along the boulevards were all coming into bloom, and there was purple verbena everywhere on the desert floor. Lemon and orange blossoms decorated the trees. People think the desert is all cactus and dirt, but when they arrive in the spring, or even the winter, they're astounded by the riot of colour. And because Palm Springs is a tourist town—or maybe just because we love beauty—you'd be hard pressed to find a single street that isn't chock full of flowers or blooming cactus or flowering bushes or trees. It made me remember my dad's theory about there being a creative force at work in the world. I couldn't help but wonder if there was a destructive force as well. We sipped our drinks and I talked to Nate and somehow we stayed off the whole miserable subject of what was happening to me for a few minutes.

Allan's place was amazing. When we reached the outskirts of A Thousand Palms we drove onto a large fenced-in property with a long, low bungalow painted a pale burnt orange set well back from the main road, and a small, neat barn nestled beside it.

Horses grazed outside in a special enclosure as two huge dogs bounded out to the car from the porch, barking, tails wagging.

"I'd like to call the airline and give them this number," I said before we left the car. "In case the planes do start to fly out."

"Please do," he said. He got out and called the dogs. "Chili! Hot Sauce!"

I made the call and, after reassuring myself that the dogs wouldn't hurt Nate, let him run around the front yard, chasing them. I sat on the front step of the house, watching as Allan ran after Nate and the dogs, making sure they were all safe. All around the property were the mountains. The sun was hitting them at an angle and they glowed almost white from the sand and rocks. It was so quiet. The world was filled with beauty—and fear and hatred. It was hard to reconcile both.

Allan took us to see the horses. Nate was beside himself with excitement, especially when Allan took him for a ride. Nate squealed with delight as they rode around the corral, making horsey noises all the way. The time seemed to fly by and before I knew it, it was lunchtime. Allan made us sandwiches—thick roast beef with dill pickles on rye bread, and a fruit salad for Nate with tiny chunks of cheese, just the right size.

Allan's cell rang. He muttered yeses and yups and uh huhs and then told whoever was on the other end that he was at his place, keeping an eye on me. He snapped it shut.

"First, Susana will be able to have visitors in a few days. She's doing much better. Second, my partner interviewed the neo-Nazi. We don't think he's in the frame—and it's unlikely he'll be back at that class after Pete's chat with him."

"You'd think," I said, "that being in the class might change his mind. Might make him realize that the Holocaust really happened."

"His type just sees it as propaganda," Allan said. "The teacher stands up in class and lies and everyone stupidly believes her."

I shook my head, marvelling at the capacity of the human mind to blindly follow an idea, never letting it go no matter what the evidence.

"I find it especially disgusting," Allan said, shaking his head. "Family history," he added. "My own."

"What do you mean?" Nate was blissfully absorbed in his food, giving us a few minutes to talk. And I was pretty keen to know more.

"Well, I was born here in the desert. My mom had me when she was older—she was forty already. I was brought up Catholic. My mother took me to services, but my dad never went. Whenever it was time to take communion, though, we'd leave. We never went to confession either. When I was little, it didn't mean anything to me, but as I got older I wanted to do what everyone else did. But Mom would grab my hand and pull me out." He paused.

"There were other odd things, too. Signs, I suppose. The furniture was always covered in plastic—in case we had to return it, Dad would say. And my parents always kept a suitcase packed in their room. Always. Anyway, I got knocked over on my bike when I was about thirteen. It happened just in front of our house. I was coming out onto the street, in between two parked cars. I didn't see the car, he didn't see me. . . . Dad saw the whole thing. He ran out. I'd been tossed a couple feet and had broken my ankle when it caught under the bike. Not too bad, considering, but it must have looked awful. My father started praying in Hebrew, what I later found out was the *Shema*."

This sounded eerily familiar. My dream! In my last dream, my "dad" had spoken the *Shema*. I tried to put it out of my head, to focus on what Allan was saying. I was pleased he was opening up. Part of me thought he was just being kind, trying to take my mind off the mess I was in. Part of me thought, or at least secretly suspected, something else. Maybe he actually liked me. Maybe he was talking to me because he felt like he could. I pushed that thought to the back of my mind. Whatever the reason, Allan was making me feel less alone, less like some stupid victim.

"Where were they from?" I asked, wanting to keep him talking.

"They were German Jews. Escaped to France before the war. They were just kids. When the French had all Jews register they became suspicious. They'd been living in Paris." He paused again. "You know the French swore up and down they'd protect the Jews. Then, after the invasion, they started to round them up. The *French* did, not the Nazis! Before the Nazis even asked. Just to suck up to them. Here's a present—Jews!" He shook his head.

"Anyway, they managed to get away. There was a little village called Le Chambon Sur Lignon up in the mountains. And they'd heard the villagers were helping people. Resistance fighters, Jews. They made it there, and were hidden by some farmers. They managed to get to Switzerland where they ended up in a work camp. After the war, when they came to California they just decided it would be better not to be Jewish any more. Safer.

"Later, I asked my father what he'd said when I'd been hurt. He blurted it all out, like he'd wanted to tell me forever. I went back to church for a few more months, but I couldn't keep it up. I was too confused. It turned out all the things I thought I was going to hell for . . . well, I wasn't. In fact, there was no hell! I couldn't deal, so I dropped the whole thing. Never really picked it up again."

"And you became a detective," I said, smiling at him. "You want to find out the truth—what's really going on." Nate was asking to get down. As I lifted him out of his chair I asked Allan if his parents ever went back to being Jewish.

"You could say so," he said. "They moved to Israel when Dad retired."

"Wow," I said. "You must miss them."

"Yeah, I do," he admitted. "They made aliyah and live on a kibbutz now. Not a religious one. They feel safe there."

"What a story! It must have been hard for you."

"It was. When you're a teenager, you want to be the one with secrets, not your parents."

The phone rang and I jumped. I'd been so absorbed I'd forgotten everything else for the moment.

Allan answered, listened and then thanked the caller. "The flights are back on for Vancouver," he said as he hung up. I almost was sorry. I mean, I wanted out of the city, but I felt so perfectly safe there. Still, I knew Allan had to get back to work. And where would we be safe then?

I started to gather Nate's things. We soon had Nate buckled into the car seat and were heading out to the airport. It wasn't a long drive. Twenty minutes later, Allan's police ID allowed us to pull right up to the front of the building.

We hadn't talked much as we drove, and when it was time to say goodbye, I was so busy getting Nate into his stroller, packing the car seat, and organizing my own bag, I barely said thanks before he drove away. I rushed into the airport and got into line for my flight. Once we'd been assigned a seat, we went to the store to buy gum. As I paid, the clerk dropped the coins on the counter and I had to pick them up and hand them to her again. She was a little slow and I sighed as she painstakingly counted them up. Finally, she handed me my gum and I turned to push Nate to the gate. There was only one problem.

Nate wasn't there.

14.

The stroller had been right beside me.

"Where's my baby? He was right here?" I cried, whirling around to look behind me, around me.

"I didn't see him," the clerk said.

"Nate!" I screamed. "Nate! Help me," I yelled at her. "Someone's taken my baby!"

I sprinted out of the store pushing bystanders aside, and looked frantically up and down the corridor. People were walking around, but Nate and his stroller were nowhere to be seen. It was as if he'd vanished into thin air. I screamed at the top of my lungs and within seconds was surrounded by security guards. "My baby," I said. "He's only a year old. He's in a stroller." I left them and began to run. I had that feeling you get when an elevator goes up way too fast and you lose your stomach. And on top of that was terror—pure terror the likes of which I had never felt before. I couldn't think. I just needed to find him. There was only one thing I knew for certain. Nate hadn't wandered off. Someone had taken him.

A guard caught me by the arm and pulled me to a stop. "Do you have a picture?"

I dug around in my purse for my wallet and pulled out a recent picture. He was wearing this adorable safari hat with a dinosaur on it, my mom had bought for him, and a matching safari shirt. He was grinning, showing his two front teeth. I handed it to the guard, wrenched my arm free and began running again, looking, desperate, desperate. . . .

And then Allan was at my side. He grabbed me, forcing me to stand still. "Ros," he said, "Tell me exactly what happened. The entire security force here is looking for Nate. You need to talk to me."

"There's nothing to tell," I wept, clutching his arm as if hanging on to it would stop me from losing my mind. "I took my eyes off him for a second, just long enough to pay for my gum. The woman didn't have the right change and she dropped some coins by mistake and I picked them up and then I turned to push Nate and he was gone."

"I'll start with the clerk," Allan said, and he strode off.

I ran into the women's bathroom; it was empty. He wasn't in the lounges either. I ran back down and checked the restaurant, the bookstore, the newsstand, the chairs. Nothing. I found Allan walking out of the store where I'd bought my gum. He shook his head. We met up with the uniforms—they'd also had no luck. Finally Allan propelled me out of the airport. I was desperate, not wanting to leave. How could I? Nate might still be there. Allan insisted. We needed to go to the police station.

Once there, he sat me in a chair and gave me a cup of hot tea. Every once in a while he'd come over with a report. As time wore on, I sunk into a state that was hard to describe. On the one hand, my heart was thudding, my pulse racing, my hands sweating as if I was in a fight. On the other hand I felt almost numb, unable to let my mind go to that place—that place where I'd start to think about what was happening to Nate right now, this second.

Perhaps so I wouldn't go crazy, or perhaps because he really thought I could help, Allan put a pad and pencil in front of me. "Jot down anything at all that you can think of that might help, anything, anyone who might want to hurt you."

I made myself focus. I needed to help Nate. I needed to not break down. I needed to be strong for him.

I thought back to when all this started with Dr. Graham's murder. Dr. Graham. I wrote down his name. And there was his wife, of course. She obviously didn't like me. Actually, she seemed to hate me, probably because she thought I'd been involved with her ex-husband. I added her name to my list. And she had three boys. Had she poisoned them against me? I put their names down as well. But to start a fire, make a car bomb? It seemed beyond the realm of simple jealousy or blame. Then there were Robert and Maureen—whose projects were being slowed down by Dr. Graham. They were probably losing tons of money. I wrote down their names. Unlike Jordan and his brothers, Maureen and Robert had the money to hire someone who knew about fires and bombs. But why go after Susana and then Nate? In other words, why go after me? Robert might be a possible suspect for Dr. Graham's death, but he hadn't even known my name until a few days ago. It made no sense. Who else? The neo-Nazi—George—from my class? Or Barbara, the right-to-lifer? What about Dr. Strong? Was this all about my work at the family planning clinic? I wrote them all down, but it still didn't make sense. Barbara had tried to warn me! And she hardly seemed to have the money it would take to pull all this off. But then, I really didn't know anything about her. That doctor—Strong—he would have the resources, the money to hire people. . . .

I *had* to come up with something. My head was spinning. I took a sip of tea. I stared at the action in the room, not really taking it in. Time passed. Eventually, Allan came over and looked at the list. He put a hand on my shoulder. I looked into his eyes, desperate to see something encouraging there—hope, maybe? "We'll find him," he said. "We will. Maybe you could call your brother? He must be worried."

I realized that he'd be frantic. But how could I tell him? I gave Allan his number and my parent's number in Australia, which I kept in my wallet, and without comment Allan took them and went away to make the calls. He returned and sat down, pulling up a chair.

"Your brother is getting a flight as soon as he can. He won't be able to come direct today and will need to go through L.A. or San Fran so he'll call when he's getting close. There was a message on your parents' machine saying they were visiting Ayers Rock and will be back tomorrow." He patted my hand, got up and went back to whatever it is they do to find kidnapped children.

Later—I don't really know how much time passed—Allan suggested that I go back to the motel.

"You can get some sleep," he said.

"I can't go back there." I was crying again, although I hadn't even noticed when the tears started to fall.

"What about Beth's? We'll have uniforms outside the house all the time. Whoever this is already knows she's your friend. We've put her and her family under protection."

I nodded, too weak to protest. He walked me to the door and motioned to one of the uniformed police, a young woman with curly short brown hair. "Jennifer will take you."

Tears trickled slowly down my cheeks as I followed Jennifer to her car. It was just getting dark, the mountains showing their silhouettes against the deep blue of the sky, lights going on, people driving home for dinner. Everything was normal, almost peaceful.

I hardly remember getting to Beth's house. I fell into her arms as soon as I walked in the door. She put me on the couch and gave me a pill and some water.

"Clonazepam," she said. "Anti-anxiety. Just take it."

I started to object.

"You can function on it," she promised. "It won't knock you out." Within minutes, I was asleep.

15.

I'm in utter blackness.

"You! How could you?"

I turn around. I can't see who is talking. The voice is a whisper, eerily familiar.

"You—you gave them my name. I was to be married next month. They've arrested Luis. We will be tortured. Our lives are over. Because of you."

"I didn't mean to," I cry. "They burned me. I couldn't help it. The pain was too great."

"I curse you. I curse you and your children and your children's children."

"I have no children," I weep. "I will never have children. I am to be burned tomorrow."

"I hope they use green wood to burn you," the whisper goes on. "Green wood. It will take longer. The pain will be unbearable. That is what you deserve."

❧

"You dreamed," Beth said.

I nodded.

"Tell me."

Still groggy, I did.

I fought the impulse to cry. I had no time for tears, or for indulging in fears and horrible imaginings. But if my dreams *were* some sort of clue, I could no longer afford to ignore them.

When I was done, Beth started to speak, her voice quiet and calm. "There's a past life therapist I've been in touch with. She told me she'd come over and do a session with you."

"Beth," I said, "I'd believe anything right now. That doesn't mean it'll help."

"Do you have a better idea?"

I didn't.

"I'll arrange it. And then I want you to eat. Something."

"It's so quiet," I said. "Where is everyone?"

"Chris has taken Lisa to a friend's," Beth said. She

didn't add, "where they'll be safe." She didn't need to.

"I'm so sorry," I said.

"It's not your fault," she answered. "But we have to find out whose fault it is."

What did the dreams have to offer? They had started just after Dr. Graham was killed. Were they predictive, or were they telling me how present events were tied to my past? Were they telling me that my past was still active in some way in my present, that there was a hatred that survived through centuries; a hatred so powerful it travelled with this soul from life to life? Was that even possible? Or was it something more ordinary, something more normal—just a dream with clues to the present? That made more sense. Much more sense.

"She'll come here," Beth said, returning from the kitchen with a plate of cold chicken and some fruit. I tried to force some food down. I spoke to Allan. There had been no sightings. Nate's pictures were all over the television and newspapers and still, nothing.

Finally the doorbell rang. The therapist arrived. She was an older woman, perhaps sixty, with white hair and glasses. She wore a dark long skirt and a long white sweater. She shook my hand and introduced herself as Bernice. We all sat down in the living room.

"Have you ever been hypnotized, Mrs. Green?" she asked me.

"No."

"And you've never done any past-life work?"

"No."

"All right," she said, pointing to Beth's long couch. "Please. Lie down. I'm going to talk to you, that's all. Hypnotism is really just a state of extreme relaxation. You close your eyes and listen. It's simple."

I laid down on the couch. I closed my eyes.

"I want you to think about your breathing," she said. "A deep breath in."

I took a deep breath. It was ragged and caught in my throat.

"That's fine. Now out."

After a few minutes my breathing sank into a more normal state. It felt like I was falling asleep, but I could hear her perfectly.

"You are looking into black. And now you see something. What?"

An image came through the darkness. It was clear and vivid, just like my dreams.

"A horse." It was odd. I knew I was talking, and yet it felt so distant, almost as if it wasn't me at all.

"Describe the horse to me."

"He's a white stallion, with brown spots. Beautiful."

"What is his name?"

"Fuego."

"Fire."

"Fuego. We fly across the grasses. We are like one when I ride."

"Where do you live?"

"With Papa and Mama and my four sisters."

"Do you live in a house?"

"Oh, yes. All white. With rose-coloured tiles. And exquisite tapestries on the walls. My dresses are white lace, as are my shawls. I love white lace."

"And is your life a happy one? Do you marry?"

"No."

"Why?"

"The Inquisition. I do not understand. They tell us we are secret Jews. I don't even know what a Jew is."

"Why are you crying?"

"They are burning Mama and Papa. My turn is next. They are hurting me."

"They cannot hurt you again," she spoke gently, softly. "You are safe now. You are just remembering. Who else is with you? Your sisters? Your friends?"

"Beth is here," I said, surprised. "She is my elder sister."

"Who else? Who are your neighbours? Your friends?"

I look around. I am at a dinner party. There is dancing—I am surrounded by dancers. I don't recognize any . . . but wait . . . yes! Maureen.

"Maureen," I said.

Maureen smiles at me, her thin face happy.

"She is my best friend."

"Your mother and father," Beatrice asked. "Who do they look like?"

I stare at them. And then it becomes clear. They look exactly like Pops and Grandma.

"Who else is there? Do you have enemies?"

I search for the faces of my inquisitors. There's one in particular, a familiar face. His blue eyes burn beneath his black hood. I gasp. It's Allan!

The phone rang just then and I awoke with a jolt. Beth answered it and motioned me over. It was Allan. I hesitated before putting the receiver to my ear. Allan: The one person I was learning to count on. Seeing him as an inquisitor shook me to the core.

"Ros?"

"Yes?"

"Someone left a note for you at the airport. It was tucked into a seat in the lounge and addressed to you."

"What does it say?"

"'*Helplessness, humiliation, then humility.*'"

"That's what it says?"

"Yes. Does it mean anything to you?"

"I'm not sure," I said slowly.

"We're checking it over for prints or anything that might give us a lead," he assured me. "What about you. How are you?"

"As bad as it gets, that's how I am," I answered.

There was a long pause at the other end of the phone. I couldn't blame him—I wouldn't know what to say to me, either. Finally, he spoke.

"We'll keep you posted," he said. "Take care." I hung up, grateful that he hadn't tried to offer any false comfort or platitudes.

I turned back to Bernice.

"Can people remember things from life to life?" I asked.

"Masters do, of course," she replied. "But not usually, no."

"Then how do our past lives affect us?"

"That's the problem," she answered. "They affect us in ways we don't understand. I often treat people with phobias and, nine times out of ten, they stem from something that happened in a past life. Fear of water — perhaps the person drowned. You know, like that. We don't realize the effect these things can have. If an extreme event has occurred, we can carry it for many lifetimes until we deal with it. You saw your friend Beth during the regression?" she asked.

"Yes."

"Also quite normal. You might think you saw her just because you know her now. More likely, you have been with her in another life, and you and she have chosen to come into this one together. Often we come back with the same close group of souls, but in different roles. Your best friend is your mother in one life, your husband the next ..."

"And can people act out anger from past lives," I asked, "without realizing why?"

"Of course," she replied. "Think about how we often have such a violent reaction when we meet someone for the first time—love, maybe hate. We wonder why our emotions are so strong. Perhaps it's because of something that happened hundreds of years ago. But to the soul, there is no time. No past, no present."

"Thank you," I said. She had given me a lot to think about.

Beatrice looked at me steadily. "I've seen the news," she said. "If the person hurting you is acting out of this terrible past, the one you just remembered, he or she will be unreasonable, full of hate. You must be very careful."

What could I say? She didn't seem to expect an answer, though. As Beth paid her and showed her out, I thought of the hatred I had seen in the priest's—in Allan's—eyes. Surely he couldn't be behind all this? Why? Even if he'd hated me in a past life, why go after me now? We were strangers before I was shot. Unless . . . unless it had something to do with Saul. They were both policemen. Was Allan covering something up? Hadn't he said his partner, whom he'd never even mentioned to me, had just come back from L.A., where he'd been investigating something? What if they *were* covering something up? Something I might have come across eventually? Shivering, I remembered how quickly Allan had gotten to the airport.

The phone rang again, interrupting my thoughts. I half expected it to be Allan, but it was Maureen instead.

"Oh my God, it's too horrible! I've seen it on TV. You poor thing! Listen, you must come over," she said. "We'll talk. You can even stay here."

"I can't," I said.

"But I've had some ideas," she persisted. "It's complicated, though, and I'd rather not go over it on the phone. Are you doing anything else? Come on. It'll be good for you, I mean, at least you won't be staring at a blank wall at Beth's."

"Anyone I hang out with is in danger, Maureen," I said. "Forget it."

"Aren't the police watching you?" she asked.

"Of course."

"So they'll know where you are. Come over. Really. I think I might know something that will help."

"Tell me then," I said.

"Not over the phone."

What was she trying to say? Did she have an idea who was doing this, and just didn't want to say anything on the phone? That's sure what it sounded like. Maybe *she* suspected Allan? I thought about Nate. I couldn't say no, not if there was the slightest chance that Maureen could help.

"Okay then. I'll be right over. What's the address?"

I glanced at Beth as I was scribbling down directions. I knew what was coming before the receiver was even back in its cradle.

"You are *not* going! Not unless you call Allan and tell him. And if you don't, I will."

"Fine." I didn't want to say anything to Beth about Allan—at least not yet.

I called him. He was puzzled, but agreed it seemed to be the only lead we had. He made me give him the address and said he might meet me there, just to keep an eye on things. He'd park down the street and I was to keep my cell on. He made me put his number on send so all I'd need to do was push a button if I was in trouble. I did as he asked.

Then I went next door and got Dad's car. And I drove towards Rancho Mirage and Maureen's house.

16.

ꟼ pulled up to the security gate at the Thunderbird Country Club, just off Highway 111. The guard called through to Maureen and then waved me ahead. I'd never been into this gated complex—one of the most exclusive in the cities. I parked in front of a bungalow with an attached double garage.

Maureen opened the door seconds after I rang the bell. She was fully made up, as always, wearing designer jeans, a white blouse, and a gaudy beaded vest. She beamed when she saw me, showing no hint of worry or concern. She certainly wasn't the most sensitive soul in the world.

"Ros, Ros, come in." She pulled me inside. "Come, sit down. I'll make coffee."

She drew me through a black and white tiled foyer into the kitchen, which was spotless, sterile, done completely in black and white. There was a large glass table and six black leather chairs around it. She pushed me into one and started to grind coffee.

"Here's the thing," she said. "Dr. Graham was involved in wildlife protection, true. But he was also about to go into a deal with me to develop a large area of land that was protected until Bush took it off the protected list."

"Why would Dr. Graham do that?" I asked.

"*Someone* was going to develop it," she said with a shrug. "I convinced him that if he were involved he could keep it environmentally friendly, whereas some others might not."

"And? . . ."

"Some of the more fanatic environmentalists got wind of it. They didn't realize he was on their side. They can be really crazy, you know. It occurs to me they may have been out to get him."

"But what would that have to do with *my* house being burned, with Susana, with Nate?"

"I'm not sure."

I stared at her, perplexed. Had she brought me all the way out here just to tell me this?

"Have you told the police?"

"No. Should I?"

"Yes, of course!" What was going on? Maureen wasn't stupid. Why ask me over just for that little tidbit. Did she just want to be near the action, as Beth had suggested, even if the action was someone else's suffering? Maybe this was exciting to her. I struggled to hold back a shudder. I wanted her to know that this wasn't a joke, or some TV show. It was real—all too real.

"Maureen, Nate is probably suffering right now, and I can't do anything," I said. "If you can throw *any* light on this, call the police. Please." I got up to go.

"It's an awful feeling isn't it?" she said, softly. "Being powerless." Then she looked up brightly. "I don't feel like that very often these days."

"No," I said, glancing around her kitchen, filled with expensive appliances and knick-knacks. "You wouldn't. Look, I really better get back."

"No, sit for a minute. There's something else."

I waited.

"If there's a ransom note. . . . I know you don't have a lot of money. I'll help you out."

"Thanks," I said, sitting back down. It suddenly dawned on me that I might just need that help. "Whoever it is hasn't asked for money. Yet. Apparently, that's a great worry to the police. It means this is not a 'normal' kidnapping. Normal." I paused. "I don't have much really. The fire took everything. There's Saul's insurance. But it's in a fund for Nate."

"Would you like a tour of the house?"

For a second, I was so taken aback I didn't answer. A tour of the house? Hadn't we just been discussing ransom notes—for my kidnapped son? I was literally stunned by her insensitivity. Nate was missing and she was offering to show me her house. And yet, she was also offering me money. I had no idea what was going on.

"I guess," I replied.

She took me into the living room first. Black leather sofas, an arm chair, large glass table on a black wrought-iron stand, small glass end tables. Coffee table books—the art of photography—all black and white.

"Nice," I lied. Allan's house had been decorated in a modern southwest style—terra-cotta colours, wood floors, with bright multi-coloured woven rugs, leather furniture. It was warm, inviting. This place was cold, cold, cold.

"I did it all myself," she stated proudly. "No decorator."

"No! Really?" This was insane, I had to get out. I'd go in a minute—as soon as the ridiculous tour was complete.

The formal dining room had a long glass table surrounded by black chairs; black and white photos of the mountains hung on the walls. We walked down a hall to the master bedroom, done, amazingly, in pink. Bright pink.

"I know it's unusual," she said, laughing as I looked around, "but I live alone. I can decorate exactly as I please!" The walls were a pale shade of pink, while the bedspread, dressers, and chairs were all shocking pink. The ensuite bathroom was done in deep purples.

"You just need to have the confidence to express yourself," she said.

The guest bedroom was pale green. "I decided that not everyone would share my taste." She smiled.

"How many kids your age are living in the Thunderbird estates?" I offered, trying to be nice. I certainly couldn't think of anything nice to say about the actual house.

"I can tell you," she said proudly. "Exactly one. Me! I'm having work done on the basement," she said as we passed a closed door in the foyer. "You can see it another time."

"Oh, I don't mind seeing a mess," I said.

"No," she said firmly, "It's dangerous down there."

She passed her hand over her forehead—a gesture that was somehow familiar. Suddenly, I remembered. The past-life regression. I'd been so distracted by Allan's appearance that I'd completely forgotten about

Maureen. She'd been there, too. Maureen had been my best friend. I felt a cold chill all over my body.

"Look, you just broke out in goosebumps," she said.

I wrapped my arms across my chest, my heart in my throat. My dream! In my dream, the other person in the cell with me had accused me of betrayal. She'd cursed me. She hated me—violently hated me. Could that friend I betrayed have been my best friend? Could it have been Maureen? And could that be reason enough to hate me now, even if she had no idea why?

Theories and ideas were swirling through my head, making it impossible to think clearly. Could Nate be downstairs? Is that why Maureen didn't want me down there? Had she invited me over just to taunt me? Should I just push past her and run downstairs? Not sure what to do, I followed her back to the kitchen. The coffee was ready and I needed to collect my thoughts. Maureen poured the steaming liquid into my mug. "Milk, sugar?"

"Lots of milk," I said. I don't actually drink coffee—it makes me sick—but that was the last thing on my mind.

"Thank you," I said, taking a sip. When I raised the cup I noticed my hand was shaking so hard that I had to put it right down again. I needed to think, quickly. Maureen's reasons for asking me over seemed to make even less sense now. They were all things she could have said over the phone. I needed to find out if she was involved. I needed to find out if she was holding a grudge.

"Maureen," I said, "I know you've probably forgotten all about this, but it's weighed on my mind for years."

"What's that?"

"The dance. You know, how Saul and I got together the night of grad. Left you out."

She waved her hand, sat down and took a sip of her own coffee. "That? Oh my God, so what? You two were obviously meant to be together. Anyway, Saul was destined to be a family man and I doubt I would like being married."

"But you must have felt terrible at the time, though. High school can be so hard."

"Well," she acknowledged, "I'd be lying if I said I wasn't mad and hurt. You know kids can be mean. That whole summer was impossible. Whenever anyone would see me they'd tease. 'Hey Maureen, been dumped lately?' Stuff like that. They even gave me a nickname: 'DD' for 'Dumped Daly.'"

"I'm so sorry, Maureen," I said. "I really am. I wasn't thinking about anyone but Saul that night."

"Of course you weren't. He was such a nice guy. Never teased me about my looks like everyone else did. I can't tell you how many times I got called 'ferret face.' But Saul always made me feel special. I guess he was just faking it," she added.

"Saul?" I said, shocked. "He'd never do that!"

"Must have," she said. "Or how could he have dissed me like that in front of everyone? If he really cared, I mean?"

"He did care. He liked you very much, but we'd been together for ages."

"Yeah, I know. But maybe he wasn't as perfect as you thought. Or as I thought. Maybe he was one of those people, pretending—pretending to be nice, and then betraying you . . ." She looked up from her coffee. "I know it must be hard for you to hear this—we like to think of the dead as perfect—but maybe it'll help you move on. After all, Saul must have had enemies or he wouldn't have been shot. So maybe he wasn't perfect after all."

I was sweating. Beads of moisture trickled down my spine. She did hate Saul. And me. "They're quite sure it was a gang thing," I protested. "Nothing to do with Saul personally."

"No one calls me names now!" she said, her eyes blank. I wondered if she'd even heard me.

"No, I'm sure they don't," I agreed, perhaps with a touch too much enthusiasm because she gave me a sharp look.

"But look at you," she observed, sweetly. "You've landed on your feet, haven't you?"

I stared at her in disbelief. My husband had been murdered, my son was missing, and one of my best friends was in the hospital. Was this landing on my feet?

"Are you nuts?" I said, unable to keep up the pretense any longer. "This has been a *nightmare!* When Saul died I thought nothing worse could happen." I paused. "I was wrong."

"Most women would have just fallen apart," she commented. "But really, the tragedy compelled you to pull it all together, didn't it?"

"I suppose." I wasn't sure what she meant. Did she think I should have killed myself or gone nuts? "I had Nate," I explained. "I had to hold it together." My eyes filled up as I spoke. "But if something happens to him—I'm not sure I could go on."

She smiled at me. Smiled. I stared at her through my tears. Was I seeing things now? And then, all at once, my thoughts started to tumble like a lock—clicking, clicking, clicking, until they clicked into place and it hit me. Could *she* have killed Saul? Was it *her*, behind *all* of this? I tried not to let anything show on my face as I went over it all. If she was capable of killing Saul, she was certainly capable of killing Dr. Graham. That would have been a double bonus. She'd have his money and she wouldn't have to deal with the hassle of his "green" concerns. And he was slowing down her other project something awful. So, she gets rid of a thorn in her side, business-wise, and has the opportunity to hurt me all over again. After all, she thought I was involved with Dr. Graham. Was I dealing with a psychopath here—a person who had no feeling for human life at all? Except her own, that is. If so, Maureen wouldn't hesitate to kill Nate in order to hurt me. She wouldn't hesitate. The reality sank in.

I got up and walked into the foyer where the door led down to the basement.

"Ros?"

I didn't answer. I needed to see if she had Nate. I opened the door, turned on the light and started down the stairs. In an instant, Maureen was right behind me.

"Ros, I said it was a mess down there. What are you doing?"

When I got to the bottom of the stairs I saw a large family room, with bright pink and purple couches, a TV, a wet bar. I spotted a couple doors. I opened one: A bathroom, all done in black. No construction anywhere.

"Ros? Are you all right? Should I call a doctor?"

I continued to ignore her and opened another door. The laundry room.

The third door opened to an empty white room. On the wall, framed, was a huge enlargement of a photo—her and Saul on the night of grad. Maureen is beaming, she looks beautiful, gazing up at Saul a look of absolute adoration in her eyes. I stared at it. For a moment, all time seemed to stand still. I couldn't catch my breath. I couldn't think. She was the one. I knew it. Suddenly, I could hear her breathing hard behind me. And for what seemed like forever that's all I could hear. I couldn't bring myself to turn around.

17.

"I suppose it's time to stop the play acting," Maureen said from behind me, adding a large sigh. "Too bad, I was enjoying it so much. You just have no sense of fun."

I whirled around to confront her. Her face was hard. Her eyes cold.

"Where is he?"

"I'll take you to him."

"Is he all right?"

"You'll just have to wonder about that."

"Will you let him go? You can do what you want with me."

"I don't know. Have you called the police? Because if you have, I'll never tell where he is."

"I haven't. They don't know I'm here. I promise."

"Fine. Let's go then."

I followed her to the garage, fighting back the urge to put my hands around her throat and squeeze and squeeze and squeeze and watch the life slowly ebb out of her, the way it must have with Saul. But I couldn't indulge myself with those thoughts or Nate would be the one to suffer. I had to think of Nate.

We got into her BMW and she screeched out of the driveway. I looked down the street. At the far end of the block, a car sat next to the curb.

Allan! He'd follow us. Everything would be all right. And I had thought it was him.

But what if Maureen noticed him? She'd never take me to Nate. My mind raced, searching for a solution. I'd have to tell her he was there to keep her trust. I didn't get the chance.

"Who's following us?"

"I'm not sure," I lied. "Maybe the police followed me from Beth's."

"You have two choices," she said, as she slowed the car down. "Stop the car, let them arrest me and never see Nate again—because I promise you I will clam up and they will never find him. He's all alone right now. You don't want him to die like that, do you?"

I could barely get a "no," out, my throat was so dry.

"Second choice: Call whoever it is and somehow

think of a way to lose them."

If I made the wrong decision, Nate would pay for it with his life—if he was still alive. I called information, not daring to call Allan on speed dial as she was sure to catch on, and asked them to put me through to the police station.

"My name is Ros Green," I began.

"Are you the mom whose son has been taken?"

"Yes."

"Hang on, ma'am, I'm patching you through to Detective Pauls. He said you might call."

How did he know I might not be able to call him directly? Maybe he'd just been covering all his bases. I was so relieved to hear his voice I almost started to cry. I bit my lip and spoke slowly and clearly.

"This is Ros Green," I repeated. "I'm calling because there is a police car following me. Please ask them to stop."

"Ros," he said, "just answer yes or no. Are you in danger?"

"Yes."

"Does Maureen have Nate?"

"Yes."

"I'll follow for a minute and then turn off as if I've just had a call. Try to keep her calm and keep her talking. I'll be nearby."

"Thank you," I said and then hung up.

"What did he say?" Maureen asked.

"That they didn't like to leave me without protection, but I insisted. Still," I added, "they'll find out I was your at house. I told Beth. They'll know it was you, Maureen."

"They'll *think* they know it was me," she smiled. "But when they find me tied up at home when this is all over, and I tell them that there was a guy in the house with a gun who made me drive you . . . well. . . . And since they aren't following us anymore they won't be able to prove any different. There," she said with satisfaction, "he's turned off."

She had planned this all out—everything—and I'd fallen right into her trap.

We were outside the grounds of her complex when she suddenly pulled over and told me to get out of the car. She leaped into a dingy old truck and told me to follow. What choice did I have? She changed direction, driving down a small lane and we were soon on the highway, well out of sight of Allan and all his good intentions.

My cellphone rang.

"Throw it out the window," Maureen ordered. "Now!"

I did, heart sinking.

She turned off Highway 111 onto Washington and then onto California Street. Finally, she pulled up to a house with a "For Sale" sign on the lawn. Her name was listed as the broker. So maybe she wasn't quite so smart—the police would be able to trace the homes she handled . . . but how long would that take? Too long, I thought. Too long. I realized I was shaking all over.

"Worried, are you?" she smiled, turning to face me after she stopped the truck. "Wondering whether you'll see his dead body? Have I hurt him? Have I tortured him? Boiling water is very effective."

Was she insane then? Why else would she consider hurting a poor little child?

"Maureen," I said, "I know you would never hurt a baby."

"You don't know anything," she said, smiling again. "Susana wouldn't agree with you."

"How could you?" I exclaimed. "She was a classmate."

"Who never gave me the time of day. Fire was just the right punishment for her."

I stared at her. I had no idea what to say to that, but Allan had told me to keep her talking. "Listen, Maureen, I know you'll think I'm crazy, but I've been having these dreams. . . ."

"Ah, so now you're a psychic." She seemed to find that amusing.

"Please Maureen, listen to me. I know you are going to find this hard to believe—so did I—but I've been having these really vivid dreams, dreams that could be showing me a past life." Maybe I could distract her. Maybe I could make her think that her anger had to do with a past life. Maybe she'd have second thoughts, or lose focus long enough so that I could grab Nate and get away from her.

She chuckled. I ignored her and kept on talking.

"I lived in Spain. And it turns out you were there. We were best friends. Beth has this crazy idea. She thinks that this whole thing, everything that's been happening, has to do with that . . ."

She interrupted me by abruptly getting out of the truck. I scrambled out and ran after her. I looked around as I followed her, trying to see if there were any neighbours around, looking for anything that might help. After all, I was a lot bigger and stronger than she was. Once I found Nate, maybe I could overpower her. Knock her out. There wasn't a soul around, though. She had probably chosen the place precisely because there would be no help.

I followed her to the front door of a small frame house. One storey, painted white, shrubs in the front, no flowers, neat, nondescript. The blinds were drawn and it just felt empty. She took a large key ring out of her purse and unlocked the door.

My heart was beating so fast it was the only sound I could hear pumping in my ears. And I was praying, I don't even know who to, praying that Nate was still alive.

The house *was* empty. There was a living room directly off the foyer, a square room with wood floors and a card table in the centre. On the table was a loaf of bread, a box of cereal, cheese, a knife, and small apple juice boxes. I forced my eyes away from the knife, purposefully not letting her see me notice it. A weapon. The food was a good sign. She wouldn't have needed food if Nate were already dead.

"Ros, if you don't stop shaking I may have to take pity on you and put you out of your misery before I tell you what's happened to Nate."

I took a deep breath. "I'm fine," I said. "Fine."

"Of course you are. Come with me."

She led me down the hall and opened a door. Lying in a crib, sleeping, was Nate. I started toward him.

"I wouldn't do that," Maureen ordered.

"Try and stop me!" I yelled. I wasn't shaking anymore. I was furious.

"Look at me!" she yelled back. I did. She was holding a gun.

Our voices had woken Nate.

"Mama," he cried when he saw me, his voice happy and excited. "Mama, Mama!"

"Hello, little darling," I said, keeping my voice calm. "Please," I begged Maureen, "just let me pick him up. Let me get him to safety. He's innocent. He didn't hurt your feelings in high school, for God's sake!"

"No. But you did. And I guess he'll have to suffer for your mistakes."

I had to stall. I had to think of a way to stop her. I had to get her talking while I thought. "Maureen how did you know I'd come over when you asked? How did you know you I'd let you bring me here? Are you sure your plan is going to work?"

"Actually, I had a number of different plans to get you here," she said. "This is good though. This was the easiest one. And, by the way, all that crap about being in a land deal with Dr. Graham was just that—crap."

I wasn't really listening. I was thinking about crazy people. Dad used to talk to me about Shakespeare's villains and what made them so believable—how Shakespeare understood their characters so well. Shakespeare, he said, thought villains had one thing in common: they craved power over others. It made them feel better, bigger. They'd lost all empathy with their victims, seeing people as objects useful only for their own gratification. Was that what was driving

Maureen now? Was I was her ticket to that pleasure? The more I grovelled, the more I shook, the more she could manipulate me, the happier she'd be? But what if I stopped? What if I refused to play? Then she'd want this game she was playing with me over quickly. I shuddered at the thought of what that could mean. I decided to quell my anger and give her what she wanted— at least until I could get the gun away from her.

I dropped to my knees. "Please, Maureen. Please. Just let me hold him. Just let me check him and see if he's all right." I let the tears flow. "Please, Maureen. It wasn't him who hurt you."

"But it hurts *you* to see him hurting," she said. "No, I think we'll just leave him. I have a lovely plan. I'm going to take both of you to an abandoned house in the Cove. You know, where all those arsons have been happening? And I'm going to tie you up and let you burn to death in the house."

"Mama! Mama!" Nate's cries were becoming more insistent. I knew that in a matter of seconds he'd be crying, wounded that I hadn't picked him up for a big kiss and a big hug.

"No one will connect me to the fire," Maureen continued. "They may suspect, but there will be no proof—nothing!"

I needed to keep her talking. I needed to get the gun. "Maureen, you have to listen," I pleaded. "I know you think I'm making up this past-life business, and I didn't believe it either, but please, listen." I continued, not waiting for her answer. "We were friends. And we were *conversos*—Jews who had converted. But the Inquisition found us out. They tortured everyone. Poured boiling water over us. Sound familiar? They burned people at the stake. Beth thinks these dreams mean something."

"They do," she replied.

"What?"

"I know all about that past life," she said with the strangest smile on her face.

"What do you mean?"

"Do you think that just because I'm in real estate I can't be spiritual?"

I didn't answer. I was beyond confused. What the hell was she saying? Now I was the one thrown off, my goal of getting the gun all but forgotten. I was so confused I shook my head, as if by doing so I could clear it.

"Do you?" she pressed.

"I . . . I . . . no! Of course you can be spiritual."

She threw back her head and laughed. "You don't get it at all do you?" she said. "You are so clueless it's almost pathetic."

Nate laughed then, copying Maureen. He thought we were all having fun. My heart almost broke.

"You're right," I agreed, "I'm clueless." And I really felt it at that moment. "So, please, clue me in."

18.

"I started having nightmares after Saul dropped me at grad," Maureen said. She held the gun firmly as she spoke. "I had what they used to call a breakdown. I had trouble leaving the house. I was worried I'd bump into someone that had been at the dance, someone who would pity me, see me as a loser. They called it agoraphobia. I started going to a shrink. One of the patients I met in group told me about this past-life therapist and how he'd helped her more than all the therapy. She was petrified of small places—claustrophobic. And she was completely cured after seeing this guy. So I went. And the first life I visited was the one you mentioned. In Spain. Where you betrayed me. And I died."

"I betrayed you? How?" This couldn't be happening. How could she be saying this? How could she know?

"Yes! I was your best friend. And you betrayed me. And now, in this life, you've done it again. You refuse to learn."

"No," I whispered, "it isn't possible!"

"What isn't possible?" she asked.

"The past-life thing," I said, "I didn't really . . ."

"Don't tell me that you didn't believe it?" she said, genuinely surprised. "That's almost funny."

"You must have been listening in at Beth's," I accused her. "How else could you possibly know this?"

"You're amazing," she said, shaking her head. "How on earth could I have bugged Beth's house? And why? Why would I assume you would talk about this to her? Your mind is so closed you can't accept it, can you? You were just using it to distract me. But here's the funny thing. It's true. It really happened."

Slowly, it was beginning to sink in. "If you and I had the same dream or vision," I said, thinking out loud, "if we saw the same thing . . ."

"Yes," she said. "Come on, Ros, you can get there."

"Then it really happened? It's true? We actually reincarnate?"

Suddenly my entire worldview shifted and rocked.

Maureen laughed again. "Why I do believe you just

saw the light! I've made you a believer!"

I shook my head, trying to think—trying to think clearly. "But I don't understand," I said, slowly. "If it *is* true, and you know your feelings about me are from a past life, why would you want to hurt me now?"

"It's a lovely bit of revenge, don't you think?" she grinned. "I get to pay you back for this life and that life, all at the same time."

"But why would you even want to? It all happened so long ago. And if you know what happened in Spain, you know I was *tortured*, that I couldn't help myself. You would have done the same."

"You hurt me in that life and you hurt me in this life and you need a lesson," she said intensely. "A big lesson. One you'll remember life after life."

"But if you hurt me, then you'll be the one who needs to make up for something," I said, grasping at anything I could think of. "I don't think karma punishes people for things that weren't their fault, but this— this is your choice, Maureen! You'll have to make it up to me in another life. Let's just be done with each other. Let's just call it quits."

"But I can't let you keep running over me like this! You didn't mean to hurt me before, you didn't mean to hurt me at the dance. For someone who doesn't mean to do things, you certainly cause a lot of misery."

"Look, I agree that what Saul and I did was insensitive. We could have waited till the dance was over. But we didn't plan it. None of it was meant to hurt you."

"Apologize. Grovel. It's all good," she said. She was still pointing the gun at me, and her face was flushed with pleasure.

She was obviously crazy. All the past life therapy had done was fuel her hatred for me. She had no feelings and she was going to kill me and Nate. I had to keep trying.

"Maureen, if you don't forgive me now, if you don't get over this, *you'll* just repeat this behaviour life after life. You live in the dark! You think that this is giving you pleasure, but it can't compare to love."

She threw back her head again and roared with laughter.

"For a Jew, you sound a lot like every minister I've ever listened to. 'It can't compare to love,'" she mimicked. "What, you think we're in some movie? You'll just say the right thing and I'll get it and we'll hug and walk out of here together? I don't think so."

But I couldn't give up. I had to try to convince her. "You don't think living with darkness, hurting people, hurts you? You may hurt me and Nate physically," I said, "but you can't take away our love."

"Ros, you are so boring, so unimaginative, so sappy. Honestly, I can't see what Saul saw in you. I really can't."

"You killed Saul, didn't you?" I stated.

"I did!"

"How?"

"I paid a gang member to do it. But with you and Dr. Graham, I did it myself. And you know, I enjoyed it much more doing it myself. Much more. The house, Susana—it was all a great challenge, but no one even suspected me!"

I stared at her and rose to my feet. I was through grovelling. I squared my shoulders and spoke, my voice loud and firm. "But you didn't kill our love," I repeated. "You can hurt me and Nate, you can even kill us, but Saul died loving us, and here you are—a lonely pathetic chick who can't love and whom no one can love back."

She moved forward then, her face a mask of fury, her hand raised, cocking the gun. I lunged at her and knocked her over backward. The gun went off in the air, but somehow, she didn't drop it. She rolled over, pointed it and shot again—not at me, at Nate. I had to stop her. I threw myself on top of her, crashing my arms down on hers so the gun whacked against the floor. It skittered away from both of us and went off again. The noise was deafening, and Nate began to scream.

Maureen was stronger than I realized, and somehow, she wiggled out from under me. I lunged for the gun as she scrambled for the door. Before I knew it, she was out of the room, the door slammed and locked behind her.

I raced over to Nate. Despite his tears, he seemed fine, unhurt. I picked him up and hugged him so hard he complained. Out of the corner of my eye, I saw the gun, still on the floor. I sighed with relief. Maureen would be too afraid to come back in here.

And then I smelled it—smoke.

Oh God, I thought. *She did it.* She had locked us up and set the house on fire, just like she said she would. This would be harder to explain away—a fire at one of her houses—but she probably she didn't care anymore. Her hatred for me had taken over all reason.

I put Nate down and raced over to the window only to discover it was boarded up. Smoke was starting to seep under the door and I rattled the handle, desperate. Nothing. I'd need to try to kick the door down. I aimed at the spot in between the handle and the lock.

I lifted my leg, then give the door a good swift kick, the kind I'd learned in boxercise class. The door didn't budge and the shock ricocheted back through my leg, almost knocking me off my feet. The knob, however, seemed to loosen. I tried again. It hurt but pain was not the issue, survival was. Again and again I kicked at the door until finally the wood splintered just above the knob. I kept at it until the frame finally shattered. I pushed the door open and the room filled with smoke.

I bent over, grabbed the gun, and then scooped Nate into my arms. We ran into the hallway, which was filled with flames. I turned to try the back door, which looked to be just beyond the bedroom. And there stood Maureen. I could only see her silhouette, and although I had her gun something told me I was still in danger. I dropped to the floor. Nate started to scream again.

Seconds later, I heard the all-too-familiar sound of a gun firing. Of course, Maureen left nothing to chance. She must have had an extra gun tucked away somewhere. I started to cough. Nate was gagging and gasping for air. I shifted him to my left arm and with my right hand I lifted the gun, aimed at Maureen's silhouette, and pulled the trigger. I'd never fired a gun. When Saul had offered to teach me, I'd refused. It kicked back a little and my arm flew up. I aimed again, fired again. She was still standing. I was starting to feel incredibly dizzy from the smoke. In minutes I'd be unconscious and she could just leave us here. I raised the gun one more time. I had no idea how many rounds or bullets were left. I pulled the trigger.

Through the smoke and the flames, I heard her swear. I saw her fall. I tried to fire the gun again, but it clicked uselessly. Empty. I had no choice. We either died by fire or by gun. I knew we had to get out.

I threw the gun away and holding Nate tight to my chest with both arms, I stood, but keeping low, crept along the hallway, afraid that at any second I'd hear the sound of a gun going off again. I could barely breathe now, but somehow I kept moving. And I asked Saul, silently, for his help. Maybe he was watching over us. Please help, I prayed. If you are there, if you can, please. I moved forward.

I couldn't see Maureen anymore. That was good, I thought, finally daring to straighten up. If we couldn't see her, then she couldn't see us.

And then, through the smoke, I saw her. She was on the floor, the gun in her hand, raised. The door was just ahead. As fast as I could, I ran straight at her, kicking at the gun as I went by. I made contact and felt it fly away, heard her cry out. I burst through the back door, Nate—coughing and gagging—clutched to my chest.

And then I saw Allan. He ran over to us, and caught Nate in his arms as I crumpled to the ground.

"She's still in there," I gasped. I could hear the sound of fire engines.

I was put on a stretcher and rolled into an ambulance. I heard Allan say not to worry, that Nate was being cared for. And then, swiftly, he bent over and kissed me, his lips just touching mine. "Thank God you got out," he said. Suddenly I felt cold and light-headed, detached from everything and everyone. Faintly I heard someone say, "She's going into shock." And that was all. Blackness.

∞

I sat up slowly. I was in the hospital again—maybe in the ER? Curtains were drawn around my bed on either side, but open to the larger space. A nurse hurried past.

"Nurse," I called out to her, my voice raspy and harsh.

"Ah, Mrs. Green. Feeling better?"

"Yes. Please, I want to see my son—Nate. Do you know where he is? Is he all right?"

"Yes, he's fine. He's in the children's ward. They're giving him oxygen and checking him for any other trauma. A Detective Pauls was here to see you and asked me tell you that as soon as you woke up."

I sighed and fell back on the pillow. How kind of him. How nice. Come to think of it . . . I sat up again. Had he kissed me? He had. I lay back again. And realized something. All I remembered after passing out was blackness. No dreams. No dreams at all. So Beth had been right. My subconscious *had* been trying to tell me something. The next time I had a weird dream, I'd pay attention.

The nurse had moved away to get some instruments. She returned, checked my breathing and my vital signs and pronounced me fine. "You can go see your son now," she said. She gave me directions to the children's ward and an extra hospital gown to cover the open back of the one I was wearing. She even handed me a pair of slippers. "They had to throw out your clothes," she explained, "because of the smoke."

I thanked her and started down the hall. My breathing still felt tight, but otherwise I felt amazingly good. And relieved. It was over. Well, mostly over. Maureen would be locked up for a very long time.

And then I saw Allan walking toward me.

"How are you?" he asked, hurrying over.

"I'm okay. What about Maureen?"

He shook his head. "She's dead."

It was terrible, but all I felt was relief.

"She did it all," I explained. "Killed Saul—well, paid to have him killed—killed Dr. Graham, set fire to my house, put the bomb in Susana's car. It's unbelievable! How could anyone be so evil?"

I thought of telling him about the reincarnation stuff—about how Maureen had come back and so had I—but I was too tired, too desperate to see Nate. That was a whole other conversation, one that would have to wait. I looked at him. It was a conversation I felt would be safe to have with him, though. I'd even tell him that he was a pretty nasty fellow in another life. But then again, I hadn't been that noble either.

He walked with me to see Nate and I told him the rest of what had happened with Maureen. I didn't mention that he'd been a suspect in my mind for a while. Now that we knew who had paid to have Saul killed, he said, the police would probably be able to find the killer.

Nate was fast asleep, an oxygen mask tight against his sweet little face. I bent over and kissed him on the forehead.

The nurse told me he'd be able to go home the next day—they just wanted to keep him overnight to make sure his breathing was all right. Would I like to have a cot so I could sleep next to him? Apparently, Detective Pauls had suggested I might want to stay.

Yes, I said. Detective Pauls was quite right. I took Allan's hand and thanked him. He sat down with me then and we watched Nate breathe. Neither of us said a word, we just savoured the peace.

I had a lot of things to think about; reincarnation, life after death, what did it all mean?

But that could wait. Nate was safe. And that was all that mattered.